MW00989714

THE PRINCESS NUN
MARY, DAUGHTER OF EDWARD I

By J.P. REEDMAN

Chapter One

When I was not quite six, I learnt I was to become a nun—and I did not believe it. The younger royal children were gathered at the manor of Langley and we were noisy and boisterous, excited at being drawn together to await the arrival of our royal parents. Father and Mama had been away crusading much of our lives, leaving us in the care of our Grandmama, the Dowager Queen Eleanor of Provence, and our army of loyal nurses and tutors.

However, our excitement spilt over into bad behaviour as I tussled, quite unladylike, with my elder sisters Megot and Joanie, over a painted foreign doll that Mother had sent to the nursery the day before. The gift was meant for me, being the second youngest girl (the baby Elizabeth was too little for such toys); my other sisters had received pretty dresses with seed pearls and soft leather boots, but no, that was not good enough, they wanted my doll too. We were tugging on it, squealing, half-laughing and half in the throes of young Plantagenet rage.

Suddenly, Joanie's unbound hair got twined around my doll's arm. As I yanked the toy away, the arm tore off the wooden body—and Joanie's deep red-gold curls went with it.

She shrieked; I thought she was going to strike me. "You're a wicked, selfish girl, Mary! I am glad you are being sent away to become a nun!"

I blinked in surprise. It was the first I'd heard of such a thing. I dropped my doll, forgotten now that the fight was won, and folded my arms defensively over my chest. "I'm not."

Joanie's dark green-blue eyes grew piggy and mean. "Yes, you are; I heard the nurses gossiping. Grandmama plans to enter Amesbury Priory and wants *you* to join her for company. You'll be stuck sitting there alone, while Margaret and I are sent to court to become proper ladies!"

"You're lying, as usual." I stuck out my tongue, looking as fearsome as a stone gargoyle carved on a church tower.

"I am not. I'm older than you and I know how these things work," she retorted, nose held high in the air. "You're going to be a nun, dedicated to the Church as younger daughters often are, but Jesu, I don't know what kind of a nun you'll make, because you…you are so wicked! Fighting like a hoyden while we are still officially mourning the death of our brother Alphonso."

"Alphonso," I murmured, gripped by a wave of unhappiness. My elder brother and, for a brief while, heir to the throne of England. He had died suddenly shortly before his eleventh birthday, sending my parents, the King and Queen, into a state of deep mourning. But it was not like they had never lost a son before; little Henry, also one-time Crown Prince, had gone to heaven earlier, much to the dismay of Grandmama Eleanor, who had nursed him herself at Guildford—not that I'd ever met Henry, for he died five years before my birth. And now there was another little baby boy in the royal cradle, destined to be King if God so willed—Edward, a cherubic, fat baby with golden curls and big eyes the hue of the sapphires in Mama's crown.

"Yes, Alphonso, have you forgotten?" Joanie gave me an imperious glare. "If you are so unmindful and so badly behaved, you'll make a terrible nun."

"I wouldn't talk about how bad *I* am," I said dangerously, casting her a dark frown. Unlike Joanie, I was olive-complected and black of brow; our large family were all different in aspect, ranging from sun-bright gold to raven darkness. "*You* spent far too long over in France with our other grandmother, Countess Joan, while she was alive. She spoilt you—that's what everyone says behind your back! She overindulged you, and you are now like a peach gone rotten. We've all seen how rotten you are. You do not even stand in rightful awe of our royal parents."

Megot began to laugh. "A peach, a rancid peach! Joanie is a maggoty old peach!"

Joanie looked as if she were about to explode in another bout of rage but instead she began to cry, a high, whining, annoying sound. "You are unfair! I miss Grandmama Joan. Why, oh, why did she die? She liked me more than you! Oh, how I hate this awful, rainy country…and it is certain I will have to stay forever. Father talks of wedding me to Gilbert de Clare, the Earl of Gloucester. He's nearly thirty years older than me and although he sends me rich gifts, I…I just can't…" Her lip wobbled, and it looked as if the whining might become full-fledged sobs.

Alarmed, Megot and I glanced at each other. For all her prettiness, for all that Grandmama Joan had coddled her, Joanie was unlucky. Our father's original intention had been to wed her to Hartman, son of King Rudolf of Germany, but the Prince, faring out by riverboat to visit his sire at Christmas, had drowned when the vessel struck a submerged rock. The impact had flung him onto a shelf of ice which had cracked beneath his weight, and his heavy wool cloak and wintry travelling robes had dragged him to his doom before any aid could be given…

Fortunately, we did not have to comfort our seemingly inconsolable and over-wrought sister, for at that moment, one of Joan's own household, her loyal nurse Edeline, strode into the chamber, throwing up her hands in dismay as she saw Joanie's red-faced, wet-eyed state. "What is all this caterwauling? Lady Joan, whatever is the matter?"

"Oh, Edeline, Mary has been so awful…" She pointed to the broken doll on the floor, its severed arm still encased in her torn-out hair.

Scowling, I folded my arms, waiting for a reprimand from Edeline, who always seemed to take Joan's side in our battles.

But today Edeline was more intent on comforting Joanie. "You must not take on so, my precious one," she soothed—making me quiver with jealousy. We all knew Joanie was the not only the favourite of our Grandmama Joan of Ponthieu, but also the favourite of Edeline—and it made her insufferable. After all, the rest of us all wanted a little bit of coddling, too.

But, I thought after a moment's reflection, perhaps I should curb my ill-feelings; after all, who would want to marry old, grizzled Gilbert de Clare, even if he was powerful and wealthy. Not me! Father had never yet spoken of my future match; thinking of Joan's blurted words about a nunnery, a sense of unease coiled in the pit of my belly. Could she have spoken the truth, that I was destined for the Church instead of the marriage-bed?

No. It could not be so. I did not *want* it to be so! I wanted to attend court with my sisters and wear fancy gowns, not end up locked away in a convent with a bunch of black crows!

Forcing my doubts to the back of my mind, I glanced back towards Joanie. Edeline was cradling her in her arms like a baby; my sister's face was less red and I could see her peering maliciously at me over Edeline's silk-swathed arm. She was going to milk our falling-out for all it was worth. Beetle-browed, wicked Mary was tormenting pretty golden Joan and deserved a good birching...

But abruptly Edeline released her charge and pushed her away. "I am tired of fighting and bad behaviour!" she said, waggling a finger at all us girls, including Joan. "And do you know why? News has come. Their Highnesses have set out from Windsor and hasten for Langley. I would die of shame if you all behaved like unruly little hellions when they arrive, instead of well-brought-up princesses. I have tried my best but…"

"It was Mary…" Joanie began to protest, her full lower lip outthrust, no longer wobbling but full of petulance.

"No, I will not brook any tittle-tattle. It is most unbecoming in a lady of quality." I stared at Edeline in surprise; clearly, with a royal visit imminent, she had grown more concerned about impressing our parents than in soothing her favourite. "Remember, you are the eldest, Lady Joan; it is for you to provide a good example to Lady Mary and Lady Margaret."

For a heartbeat, I thought Joanie would burst into a full-fledged tantrum—but by some miracle sent from Heaven, she managed to control her emotions. Instead of screaming, she merely threw back her mussed hair in a haughty gesture. "You are right, Edeline. I must show appropriate deportment to the unruly little *children*…Now, come, help me choose my dress for when Mother and Father arrive!"

She stalked out of the chamber, Edeline hard on her heels chattering about how blue and silver were good colours…but what about green to bring out the colour of Joanie's eyes?

Megot rushed over to me and clasped my hands excitedly; her fingers were hot and sticky from the barley sugar she'd been eating—a gift from Grandmama Eleanor who gave us lots of such treats. "Mary!" she squealed. "Isn't it wonderful? Mama and Papa are going to visit us at last!"

Her excitement was infectious; I squeezed her fingers hard and we danced around the room, our long hair whirling, mine dark as night, hers the colour of autumn leaves.

"Yes!" I cried as we fell into a happy heap. "It is marvellous, like a dream—a wonderful dream!" *As long as Joanie was lying and they wouldn't come for me with a nun's habit...*

The next few days were full of activity as our clothes for the grand occasion were chosen and we were drilled by Edeline and our other governesses, nurses, tutors and even a bishop as to what we must say and do when our royal parents arrived.

Towards the end of their long-winded sermons about deportment and behaviour, I grew rather bored; the servants in the house below were panicking, rushing noisily about with buckets to get the flagstones spotless, while the courtyard was filled with shouting, grunting carters hauling in supplies for the royal visit. Always short-tempered at even the best of times, the steward was bawling at the household staff, trying vainly to keep all in order. I just wanted to get away from all the noise and the balding old bishop with his wobbling jowls, who was lecturing us on honouring one's parents.

But peaceful rest was not to be, even when the bishop finally shuffled away, his preaching done. I was set upon by a gaggle of nursemaids, scolded for my inattention, then dumped in a bath of barely tepid water. Afterwards, they wrapped me in red velvet and taffeta and pressed a golden band upon my forehead. My long near-black braid hung behind me, twined with satin ribbons.

It was while I whined and complained about the itchiness of the circlet and had my hands slapped as I fiddled with it, that I heard horns wildly blowing from outside the window casement. Mother and Father had reached Langley at last!

Pulling away from the nurse who was trying to straighten my circlet, I rushed to the window and hurled the painted shutter open with a noisy clatter. Below, the courtyard was a riot of colour and activity; pennants snapped in the breeze, the leopards of England snarling, golden and ferocious, the castle of Castile dancing against the clouds like a fairy-tale fortress.

"Come away, Lady Mary!" cried the nursemaid, dragging me back from the bright tableaux beyond. "Their Graces would be scandalised if they saw a daughter hanging from one of the tower windows!"

Sulkily I retreated and sat upon a little stool. "When can I see them?" I moaned, hugging my knees to my chest.

"When you are called," said the beady-eyed nurse severely. "Patience is a virtue—and you must learn it, Lady Mary."

Grumpily I sat down and chewed the end of my braid. Virtue…such a dull word, for dull sorts of girls.

The sun had started to slip westwards and the chamber turned rosy and then sullen yellow before I was finally summoned to my parents' apartments. Mama's favourite lady-in-waiting, Margery de Haustede, appeared at the door, a tall, spare woman in rich attire, her fair hair confined in a silver net. "I have come for the Lady Mary," she announced, glancing towards my nurses.

I was on my feet in an instant, exuding excitement from every pore, virtually bouncing in my new, jewelled slippers. "Now, Lady Mary," Margery scolded. "You must remember to have decorum as befitting your station. You are entering the presence of the King and Queen, not cavorting in the nursery with other children."

Together Margery and I walked down the newly-built Queen's cloister, burning with flambeaux that made the shadows dance. Ahead, I could see courtiers streaming in and out of the rounded arch that led to the Great Hall. Musicians were playing winsome airs on lutes and dulcimers, and the fragrance of heavy incense hung in the air, reminding me of chapel.

I made to go toward the Hall but Margery shook her head and pulled me back by the sleeve. "No, Lady Mary, the feasting and merriment will come later; first their Graces want to see you on your own."

Despite being flushed with excitement, I also felt a nervous thrill. Perhaps rumours had reached my parents of squabbles with Joanie, or some of the other infractions I'd committed—dropping my Psalter in the mud, learning chess when I should have been practising embroidery, trying to climb onto the humpy back of the pet camel that we had in our own little menagerie.

I was grave-faced as I was taken further down the torchlit passageway to my mother's private apartments. When Margery and I finally reached the door to mama's chamber, I was told to wait and Margery went in, leaving me jigging nervously from foot to foot in the corridor.

The door hung open a crack and I could hear my parents talking…no, they were closer to arguing. This was a shock to me, since my parents were very close, despite my Father's known stern nature. He reserved most of his ire for the battlefield and his enemies; if we displeased him, we would certainly know it, but he indulged us all in ways that surprised many.

"I do not know if we do the right thing, Ned," said Mama, her voice with its rich Spanish overtones sending a thrill through me. It had been so long since we'd last met, or so it seemed to a girl not quite six. "She is young yet, so young."

"We made a promise, Leonora." Father called Mama by her old Spanish name which she had dropped in order to sound more English. The folk of England were not much enamoured with foreign Queens, as both Mother and Grandmama Eleanor had discovered. "A promise to send a daughter to the church. It is one we must keep. Remember how Gila, the Prioress of Fontevrault hounded me to send the girl to join the order? She almost threatened me. *Me*, the King of England." I heard the shadow of outrage in his voice.

"To think, our Mary sent abroad to Fontevrault; the French might abduct her from the cloister and use her as a weapon against us," said Mother, voice heavy, almost tearful.

I swallowed hard. So, Joanie's words were not just tittle-tattle. They were horribly, irrevocably true. My parents had vowed me to the church and I would be sent away…

There was a rustle at the door. Margery peered out, the silver wires in her headdress glittering in the torchlight. "It is time, Lady Mary. Their Graces will see you."

Almost reluctantly, I entered the chamber, blinking back unwelcome tears. My excitement had withered like a plucked lily. But I was brave, I was a Plantagenet and the daughter of a Crusader King. A King feared by other Kings. I walked forward with my head high and my lips drawn into tight lines to keep them from quivering.

Into the centre of the room I went. The surrounding space was well-lit by candles held aloft by bronze candelabrum. On one wall, painted flowers violet, blue and red shot up from green shoots twined together like serpents; on the other, St Katherine was martyred on the Wheel, her crown shooting rays of holiness, the Wheel's spokes throwing flames to burn those who martyred her. Beneath my feet, coloured tiles glimmered in swirls and spirals; imported Spanish rugs lay thrown about randomly to give added warmth. Two high, thin windows allowed in light and air; they were filled with delicate grisaille glass, as grey and filmy as morning mist. Being Mother's chambers, many of her prized possession were on display—precious leather-bound tomes about King Arthur, a fine marble chessboard, coloured glass vases from Venice through which the candlelight welled, turning them into glowing, magical receptacles of colour.

Amidst all this opulence, my parents sat before a little stone-topped table, on chairs carved from dark wood. Silver plate was spread before them; on her travels Mama had purchased knives with hilts of green jasper, and they gleamed green upon trays filled with imported foodstuffs—sun-yellow lemons, sugar-dusted figs and fat red pomegranates cut in half, their seeds oozing bloody juices. Next to them were blocks of doughy, white cheese, which had come from the French lands of my Uncle Edmund's wife, Blanche of Artois.

Mother was plump, as I remembered her, soft and round from her many pregnancies; her deep brown hair was wound in braids covered by a translucent veil adorned with sparkling stones. Her usual placid smile was missing, however; she looked disturbed, her eyes big and dark, circles ringing them as if she had not slept well.

Next to her, my Father was impressive and fearsome, a King amongst Kings. They called him 'Longshanks' and so he was—you could tell even as he sat—his long, lean legs were stretched out before him, encased in boots of Spanish leather decorated with gold studs. He had a sharp, thrusting jaw and hair that appeared dark in gloomy places but lit up with red and gold when sun or torchlight stroked it; he had near-white hair as a child but it had deepened through his life almost to the complete opposite. His eyes were an icy blue and perhaps his most terrifying feature, piercing the subject of his attention like a pair of keen lances. One eyelid drooped, which may have given other men so afflicted a sleepy, comical look. But not my Father, that lowered eyelid gave him a sinister air, as if it covered the evil eye, as if it shielded his true thoughts, so often mirrored unwittingly in a man's eyes. That was my Father, stern as a castle wall, unbreachable, firm as iron—warrior-prince and scourge of the Welsh.

"Mary…" Mother who spoke first. "Have you no greeting for your parents?"

I had been so stunned by learning the truth of my future, spoken when I was not meant to hear, that I had grown dumb, like some poor invalid sequestered in a hospital and cared for by monks' charity. Immediately, I forced myself to act as required. Affecting a rigid smile, I bobbed a deep curtsey before the two seats.

Once I had risen, Mama beckoned me to her, inspecting my person as if she thought a sorceress might have waved a wand over me in her absence and transformed me into some hideous, wayward creature. Her worried frown deepened; she bit on her full lips. "Husband, just look at her. Still so young. Too young."

Father was imperious, as ever. "Mary will be in good hands at Amesbury. My mother the Dowager Queen shall oversee and make sure all is well. What do you say to that, daughter? Life as a nun of Fontevrault with your grandmother?"

I knew I was expected to curtsey and simper and acquiesce with all good graces. But there was always an outspoken streak in me, like that which had occasionally flared in my Grandmama Eleanor in her youth, and I said, most plaintively, "Must I become a nun, your Grace? I would rather not."

Mother looked shocked at my forwardness. Father…I would not have shown surprise if those frigid blue eyes had turned a demonic red. I saw a muscle jump in his cheek. "Does it need explaining to you, Mary?" he said in a frigid voice. "Younger children are often given to the church. We have decided to offer you, child. What you make of your life in the cloister will be up to you." He laughed and it was not a pleasant sound. "I do not intend to find a husband for you; as if anyone would wish to wed such a wilful maid, be she royal or no."

"Edward!" Mother cast him a reproving glance, which he ignored—and then she turned to me, consoling. "Do not worry, Mary, not only will your grandmother and cousin Eleanor dwell at Amesbury to keep you company, we will visit as often as we may. And you will not be cloistered, locked behind walls with no access to the outside world; St Mary's Priory is not like that. Even when you've taken your full vows, you can still come to court. Isn't that right, husband?" She raised her warm brown gaze to my father, pleading.

A corner of his mouth moved; was…was he trying to smile? "Mary is my daughter and has a look of determination about her; I do not think even I should manage to stop her. Now, child, go…you are dismissed." He snapped his fingers and summoned a page to fill his goblet with wine.

I stood gawping for a moment and when he turned back towards me, the half-lidded eye looked more baleful than ever and that ghost of a smile had vanished like morning mist. "You still here? I told you, girl…you are *dismissed*."

I ran.

Chapter Two

Leaving Langley was a sad day. As if in a sorrowful dream, I drifted through the newly-paved cloister and the garden with its exotic water features placed on the terraces by Mother's design. Apple trees stood proudly, their boughs heavy with budding fruit; the 'viniator' James Frangypany was whistling as he trimmed their branches with fearsome-looking shears. A little further away, gardeners shipped in from Aragon hewed at hedges and tended flower beds and ponds, some singing in Spanish as they worked. I raced over to their master, Ferdinand Ispannus, who was digging a shallow ditch, his crinkled face shadowed by a broad hat—although there was little sun that day. It was a custom he had brought from Spain where the weather was often hot.

"Hola, Ferdinand!" I cried, waving my hand.

He stood up immediately, set his spade aside, and gave a little bow with hand on heart. "Lady Maria."

He always called me Maria, which he said was what they would call me in Spain. I liked it; the name rolled off the tongue much better than Mary. "I am coming to say farewell, Ferdinand. I am going far away to become a nun."

"So I have heard, little Lady Maria. You will serve the Mother Maria from now onwards. Here—this is from me and all the Spanish gardeners of Langley to you… for Remembrance." He cut a sprig of greenery from a nearby rosemary bush and pressed it into my hand.

Feeling my eyes fill, I forced a smile. "Thank you, Ferdinand. I must go now. I must say my goodbyes to Saladin."

Sprig of rosemary clutched in my hand, I hurried through the garden to the stable; passing the fine horses with their nodding heads hanging out of their stalls, I entered the little bestiary built outside the back of the building.

Sorrow in my heart and a tear standing in my eye, I stroked the nose of Saladin, our old camel brought long ago from paynim lands, whispering a heartfelt adieu—and he spat at me. *Evil beast*, I thought, wiping foul-smelling spittle from my cheek. I had always treated him well even when the other children ran rampant, clambering over his humps as if they were mountains!

I left Saladin, who seemed unbothered by my departure, and plunged into the nearby Kennels, where I rubbed the wet, inquisitive noses of the gathered hounds, letting them cover me with wet farewell kisses. I then, purely by chance, bumped into Megot who had escaped her tutor and was lurking behind a pillar. It was there my wild run ended, for the tutor was hot on Megot's heels and hence both she and I were undone. Scolding ensued and we were both marched into the house as if we were prisoners—which, I felt, we were. Or at least I was.

Edeline appeared, expression annoyed. "Lady Mary, the hour is growing late," she barked. "The entire household has been searching for you!"

I was hastily wrapped in rabbit-skin travelling robes and guided firmly to the courtyard with its ornamental tiles and little pools with spraying fountains. I kissed the two babies, Elizabeth and little Edward, who had been carried from the nursery to witness my departure. Elizabeth, the elder, began to whimper, while Edward gave a blood-curdling howl and pounded the air with curled fists. I did not know if that was because they sensed their dear sister would soon depart or because, as Joanie often said, my black-browed look scared babies…and dogs…and even other children.

A chariot stood next to the courtyard arch, waiting to bear me hence to distant, mysterious Amesbury. Footmen and soldiers swarmed around like a hive of angry bees, busy with preparations for my departure. The whole household filed out of the manor house to see me on my way; I wondered if they were sad or glad to see me go.

As I stepped towards the chariot, Joanie flew from the door of the house and rushed up to me. To my surprise, tears trickled down her cheeks. "Oh, Mary, I will miss you!"

"You will?" My dark brows lifted in surprise until they vanished under my long, unruly fringe.

"Of course I will," she said, lips quivering as they always did when she was upset. "I'd even give you that doll you liked—but they wouldn't let you have her in that stuffy old priory."

I narrowed my eyes, tempted to remind her the doll was intended for me from the very start. "Thank you anyway for the thought, Joan," I said sarcastically. "I pray you keep well…Did Father say anything about your wedding to dear old Gilbert? Maybe they'll let me out of the nunnery to wish you both well."

Joanie looked stricken; she obviously did not wish to speak of her betrothal. "Oh no," she said, not answering my slightly spiteful question, "but they won't let you out of the priory for a wedding, Mary, you goose. You'll be locked in there, singing and praying…"

"Don't you count on it, Joan," I murmured. "Mother promised…"

Sharp fingers tapped me on the shoulder. Edeline. "Lady Mary," she said with sternness, "it is time to go. We must be on the road. The Prioress awaits your arrival in Amesbury; thirteen daughters of nobles will become novices at the same time as you, but you will be pre-eminent over them all. *You*, as the daughter of the King…seconded by your cousin, Lady Eleanor, who already resides at Amesbury and had been veiled."

Eleanor. I wondered what she would be like. Although her father John was Duke of Brittany, Eleanor's birthplace was in England. Her mother was my Aunt Beatrice, Father's younger sister, and they were close as children. Eleanor, being a few years my senior, was never a childhood playmate, however. We had met only once, at a great family gathering; she had seemed mousy and reserved. Nothing else was memorable about her.

"Mary!" Edeline's voice was insistent. "Hasten! Did you not hear a word I said?"

Grabbing my skirts with both hands, I clambered ungracefully into the chariot and thudded down onto the cushions piled on the wooden seat. Edeline crawled in afterwards, tutting. I twitched back the curtains to take one more look at my siblings.

The babies were still crying, kicking and twisting in their nurses' stout arms. Margaret was playing with a stray hound; she looked a bit sad but she did not glance up, despite me willing her to. Joan was already racing back in the direction of the manor house door without a single backwards glance.

I settled myself on my seat, attempting to get comfortable for the long journey ahead. Maybe, even at my tender age, it was indeed time to leave childish things behind and accept the lot of a younger royal daughter. By the time the carriage rolled past the outer lodge known as Little London and lurched onto the trackway beyond, I was already thinking of what my future might hold.

Amesbury was a small town in Wiltshire. The Benedictine Priory, daughter house of Fontevrault, had been raised by my great grandfather Henry II in atonement for the murder of Becket, who was smitten dead in his own cathedral by a posse of great, lumbering knights who had more brawn than wits. At the same time, the older abbey, founded by an old Saxon Queen called Aelfthrith, was decommissioned and given to the town for its own use. Grandmama Eleanor had always borne a liking for the place as she rode between her other favourite properties at Marlborough, Ludgershall and Clarendon, and hence decided on the priory for her retirement—although she was not quite ready to join the sisters yet. First, she was having special quarters built at the priory for her own private use. I was to receive the same, on a smaller scale.

Intrigued by my new hometown, I stared out the chariot window, despite Edeline scowling and muttering that it was inappropriate for a young lady of worth to gawp at peasants like some kind of simpleton. I ignored her admonishments.

Outside, a rutted street ran through the heart of a small but busy town. Carts filled with straw, wool and tuns of ale wheeled away out of our path. I noticed a pig-boy with a shock of orange hair and mud-smeared cheeks birching his porcine charges through the teeming gutters; he spied me too, grinned a cheeky gap-toothed grin and tipped a ragged cap. I blushed furiously.

"I told you," said Edeline primly. "Ladies should not stare out at the commons."

We proceeded onwards, as the townsfolk arrived to gape and heralds blew horns to announce the arrival of important persons. To our right, we saw the priory guest house, grey and great-walled, its doors disgorging the relatives of the noble girls who were to become novices today.

Passing onwards, I spied a huge church. I thought it surely must be Amesbury Priory, but Edeline told me that it was the first monastic house built there, and that our destination, St Mary's, lay out in the fields behind the older foundation. Turning sharply before the imposing building, the chariot trundled down a long, winding track toward a smaller and more intimate-looking church, with a tall, thin spire and handsome outbuildings that shone in the wan sunlight.

"So this is to be my home for the rest of my days," I said wonderingly. It looked peaceful, at least. It seemed a strange thought that I had to stay here and would never again spar with Joan or feed the hounds with Margaret.

Once the chariot had rolled into the priory courtyard, I was handed out by attendants. A young nun with a white oval face and warm eyes approached. "I will take you to Prioress Ida, Lady Mary," she said. "I am Sister Laurencia; I am in charge of the novices. Is there anything you require before we meet the Prioress?"

"Could I change my dress?" Dust had blown over my clothes because I had insisted on hanging from the window; my hair was a raven snarl about my shoulders.

A little smile touched Sister Laurencia's lips. "That won't be necessary, Lady Mary. The Prioress has all the garb you'll need."

I was led away from Edeline. "Be good," she murmured at my retreating back. "Do not shame your lovely mother, the Queen, whom I love like a sister."

That admonishment ringing in my ears, I followed Laurencia's dark habit through a serene cloister surrounding a garden and then up a flight of curved stairs into the chapter house, where sunlight streamed through painted glass and released a riot of colours over Biblical murals and alabaster statues of the Virgin and Christ.

The Prioress of St Mary's was standing amidst the light, an older woman with a face that appeared kindly, almost motherly. Other nuns flocked around her, holders of various positions in the nunnery—some looked gentle and mild, while others were imperious and a little frightening in their robes of stark black and white.

Prioress Ida extended a hand but did not touch me. "Welcome, Lady Mary. We have been waiting for you. I trust your journey was uneventful?"

I nodded.

Ida gestured to Sister Laurencia. "Get the Lady Mary the robes of a novice."

"At once, Lady Prioress," murmured Laurencia and with a slight bow, she exited the chapter house

While we waited for her return, Prioress Ida told me of the ways of the priory which I must learn in the days to come. "Your gracious father, his Grace the King, has given you an income of £100, a goodly sum. You can obtain what you need, when you need it, from Sister Treasurer." She nodded toward a portly nun whose body strained against a too-small habit. "As you probably are aware, we are in the process of building quarters for the arrival of your esteemed grandmother, the Dowager Queen. You, too, are to reside in quarters separate from the rest of the nuns, as befits your rank; your rooms are already prepared."

I hardly heard the words about my quarters. £100! My head was spinning. I could buy dolls or sweet things or a little hound...Oh, no, I couldn't anymore; not in a convent...Or...or could I? Maybe just a little?

"Sister Agathe is the Sacrist." Ida went on, pointing to a tall, spare sister with an eagle's beak for a nose. "She cares for the plate and for the church itself. If you note any tallow candles burnt to stubs or any leaks in the roof when it rains, you must it report to her."

"I shall, Mother Prioress," I murmured.

"Here with me also is the Chantress, Sister Immaculata. She is in charge of music and singing. Can you sing, Lady Mary?"

I flushed to the roots of my hair. "Not really. My sisters say I sound like a crow being strangled."

Prioress Ida choked back what was clearly a peel of laughter. "Well, not to worry, child. You won't be the first, and it matters not. God gave you that crow's voice, after all. How about books? Have you interest in books?"

"I am just turned seven, Mother Prioress, but I am learning my letters and I do enjoy looking at the painted pages."

"Of course. A good start. Sister Immaculata is also the Librarian of this House. She will guide you towards reading our treasured manuscripts when you are ready, which I have no doubt will not take long. I have heard you are a clever child, and Sister Laurencia is an excellent teacher."

At that moment, Laurencia returned, bearing in her arms my new robes, in the stark colours that I would most likely wear for the rest of my days. Yes, I was only a novice at present and could leave the priory until my final vows were taken, but unless my sisters should all die, I would not be required for a marriage-alliance, and it was customary and deemed honourable for Kings to give spare girls to the Church.

Carefully I took the garments from Sister Laurencia; they were heavy, of thick, dyed wool. I almost stumbled beneath the unexpected weight, for I was neither very tall in height nor very strong.

"Laurencia will take you to your quarters," said Prioress Ida. "You will gather with the other new novices later this afternoon to swear obedience to me and to this House. Besides the Mistress of the Novices, you will have another helpmeet to help you adjust, the Lady Eleanor, your dear kinswoman."

A rustle of robes sounded on the tiles behind me. I turned to see my cousin standing in the arch of the doorway. She hadn't changed much from how I remembered her, although now grown quite tall—a mousy girl with a pale complexion and brows and lashes so fair the light coming through the windows made it look as if she had none.

She gave me a look and my heart sank. I do not know if it was apparent to Prioress Ida or Sister Laurencia, but my 'dear kinswoman' was making it rather obvious—my cousin of Brittany had no liking for me.

Chapter Three

I adjusted to convent life more easily and more quickly than I had expected. I frequented the library often, under the pleased eye of Sister Immaculata, who brought out books she thought appropriate for me to look at. (Behind her back, I sometimes skipped to images of martyred saints, not because I was particularly dedicated to their cults but through a child's slightly prurient curiosity.) She also quizzed me on my singing—'Is it true, Lady Mary, that you cannot sing a note? Or are you just shy? Let me hear you sing! I am sure I can teach you."

I opened my mouth slightly. "Aaaaaa…" A horrible grating noise filled the library. I swear the narrow glass windows high above shivered a little.

Sister Immaculata's face scrunched up as though she was in pain. "Ah, so you were telling the truth. Never mind. You can just open and close your mouth at the right times when Masses are sung. As long as you know the words and their meanings, God—and I—will be satisfied."

The worst part of my new life was Cousin Eleanor. I tried to befriend her but it was like chipping away at the ice on a frozen river. Perhaps she resented a new royal cousin at the nunnery; I never did find out the true reason for her animosity. But it was there and never changed from the first day onwards.

It did not help that Eleanor was Holy—completely immersed in her new religious life and dreaming of being a powerful abbess in the distant future—while I was, to her eyes, more like a *Holy Terror*.

I said the prayers, I did the devotions—but Amesbury town was new to me and I wanted to explore the area around the priory, much to Eleanor's disgust. She could not see why it mattered and thought it crass and unseemly that I should want to see the profane world and not spend all my time counting rosary beads or asking forgiveness for sins I hadn't really committed.

I would have been happy to leave her in the priory while I fared outside with other nuns, but because Prioress Ida had entrusted me to her special care, Eleanor dutifully trundled after me wherever I went, mouth pursed as if she had sucked on a lemon imported from Mama's homeland of Spain.

Like my grandmother, Eleanor of Provence, I had a keen interest in the legends of King Arthur. Queen Guinevere was rumoured to have entered a convent in Amesbury, and although it could not be St Mary's or even the older abbey of St Mary and St Melor, it had to have stood close to the very spot I dwelt. So I desired to try to find traces of the great Queen within the priory's expansive parkland and the little town beyond.

First stop was the old abbey near the town's main road and the ford. Inside, a beautiful pane of stained glass of a golden-haired lady gleamed in one high, pointed window; with much reverence, the locals referred to the figure as 'Guinevere.' Excited, I pointed her out to Eleanor; my cousin sniffed and said in a chilly tone, "That's not Guinevere, you dunce. It's a depiction of the Virgin Mary."

I frowned and glanced toward the high altar, adorned with the relics of young St Melor, a princely boy-saint of Brittany who was murdered by his wicked Uncle Riwal. His skull grinned at me almost impishly. I fought back the urge to grab it and bounce it off Eleanor's head; I didn't think Melor would mind, for he was a little boy as well as a saint and little boys did things like that and found them humorous. But I restrained myself and lit a candle in his shrine, wondering if I could 'accidentally' catch the end of Eleanor's habit with the flame…But those were wicked, unworthy thoughts and I did not act on them.

Next, we wandered down by the river Avon, winding like a snake through the fields. Eleanor was white and breathless, gazing fearfully at the dark hump of the tree-bound hill on the far side of the running water as if she thought fearful brigands would come leaping down from the heights to carry her off. (I rather wished one would but I would pity him.)

Ignoring her, I happily stripped off my shoes and started playing in the water; the Avon was quite a mysterious place, for I noticed that the be-slimed rocks beneath my white toes were coloured royal purple.

"Mary, you really should not be doing that!" frowned Eleanor, folding her arms. "Showing your bare feet!"

"Showing them to whom? The fish?" I teased. "Or maybe a frog?"

Eleanor's face mottled. "The road is not far away! There might be some village oaf *looking*."

"Then let him look!" I called over my shoulder as I hoisted up my heavy skirts and darted away along the riverbank into the deepest, darkest tangle of trees, where the river opened into a wide, sullen pool, flies and bugs skimming over its surface.

It was a strange place; an odd silence hung over it and a stillness; the water scarcely moved but long white tendrils coiled from it like the hair of ghosts.

Eleanor crossed herself. "We should not be here. This is a bad place; I can feel it."

"Bad in what way? It's a pool."

"It…it is *demonic*; can you not feel it? Oh, Mary, come away…"

I had to admit I felt *something* in that lonely place but I wouldn't tell my cousin that. I doubted the 'something' was demonic, although the countryside from here to Northumbria was rife with legends of water-trolls and green-toothed witches that reached out of the weeds to catch unwary children and drag them down to doom.

Ignoring Cousin Eleanor, who was by now chanting a Hail Mary and rocking in distress, I wandered a bit further around the edge of the pool. At one point, the neighbouring bushes grew thicker, twining about the remains of some kind of a structure. Filled with the spirit of adventure, I walked over to it, putting my shoes back on to protect my feet from the thorns that grew in abundance.

To my delight, I seemed to have stumbled on the foundations of an ancient building. There was a rectangular paved floor and the crumbled remnants of walls, all snarled with copious vegetation. If there had ever been a dome covering the structure, it had long collapsed, for it lay completely open to the sky and the elements. The pavement was damp, streaked heavily with green; it appeared that on occasion the adjacent pool would ebb and flow, covering the floor of the tiny house. The remains of a doorway was situated precisely so that flooding could occur.

My childish mind went wild, as I envisioned Queen Guinevere slipping away from the nuns to bathe here—and to think back on Lancelot and the wrong she did to her husband, Arthur. Maybe even to *meet* the great knight, to embrace him one more time, to kiss…

"Do you think Guinevere might have come here?" I blurted, forgetting in my rapture that my companion was the dull, unimaginative Eleanor. "See where the water comes in? It must be a healing shrine, an ancient healing shrine. Oh, how I wish I could strip my robes off and bathe here as she might have done centuries ago!"

"And be bitten by midges and goodness knows what else!" Eleanor stared at me as if I'd gone mad. "You must stop this childish daydreaming, Mary. That Queen Guinevere was a wicked woman, an adulteress! You know what *that* means, don't you? She was a harlot! Come away now, or I shall have to tell Sister Laurencia of your bad behaviour!"

"You wouldn't dare! I've done nothing wrong!"

"I said, *come away*!" She grasped my sleeve, her skinny fingers like pincers.

Instinctively, I fought to free myself by giving her a hard push—harder than I thought. With a high-pitched shriek, Eleanor stumbled backwards and fell on her bottom in the shallows of the pond.

I tried to help her up, suddenly repentant, but she flailed at me with her arms. "Get away, Mary. I wish you had never come here! You'll never fit in; you'll never be a proper nun—that is clear to all!"

I put my nose in the air. "If that is true, so be it. I am not like the other nuns here anyway. I am a princess."

"You need to forget your birth! You must become humble in the eyes of God and man!"

Shoulders stiff, I stalked away from her, my day ruined. I would not let her hurt me, fill me with fears. If I did indeed end up a failure of a nun, it was not my fault—for in my heart of hearts I knew I could not be other than I am…

Chapter Four

Thankfully, Cousin Eleanor stopped dogging my every step after the incident at the pool. Whether she had told Sister Laurencia or the Prioress, I never learnt, but I was never taken to task for misdoings. I did not care much anyway. I was excited. I was looking forward with great anticipation to the arrival of my beloved family. They were coming to collect me and then we would ride on to Dover to greet Grandmama Eleanor, who had been visiting her kinsfolk on the continent before going into retirement at Amesbury

It would be a grand Plantagenet party.

My heart beat like a drum when I finally heard the trumpets of their entourage blaring as they entered Amesbury. Lined up at the head of the other novices, with Cousin Eleanor glowering beside me, I watched with familial pride as the royal party processed past the town church and down the beaten pathway leading to the Priory of St Mary.

Knights in polished armour took the fore, bearing standards; lilies burst out white against the cerulean sky and leopards leapt snarling in the wind that crossed the wide plain beyond the town.

Father then appeared, riding on a bay destrier caparisoned in deep, rich blue silks fringed by golden tassels. His cloak was scarlet, decked with star-shaped gems, and he wore a ceremonial crown and spurs of gold. Mother followed on a mannerly white palfrey with silver bells plaited in mane and tail; sapphires blazed on her netted headdress and her voluminous gown, azure as the heavens, fluttered in the breeze. My sisters and brother were in a large carriage draped in silver streamers, trundling along near the rear amidst crowds of richly-garbed attendants including musicians who played jaunty airs as the entourage moved with graceful majesty toward the priory.

My heart told me to run forward, but knew I must have dignity as befitted both a princess and a nun. Father and Mother dismounted and greeted Prioress Ida, and then the rest of the royal children disembarked. I tried to make eye contact but only Elizabeth dared to break protocol and smile back at me as a grand procession went to the priory church for a thanksgiving Mass.

For a few hours, I chaffed and shuffled in my itching robes as Masses were held and declarations made. I mouthed the words in the singing in church and beside me, Cousin Eleanor roared out the hymns with warbling gusto—louder than usual, I thought—clearly trying to show off before her aunt and uncle.

Later, the notables gathered in my private quarters. Finally, I was free to greet my family. Megot and I hugged and kissed, Elizabeth and Edward fawned upon me like puppies; even Joanie seemed pleased to see me and said, her big green-blue eyes filled with sincerity, "I have missed you, you know. Even our fights. It seems so quiet at Langley without your chatter." My oldest sister, Eleanora, had joined the party too—as the eldest, she had not lived with the rest of us at Langley—she was already at court with Mother learning a lady's ways. Tall and regal, her long green dress was spangled with silver buttons; baby Edward kept grabbing at them, attracted by the sparkle.

As a close relative, Cousin Eleanor was permitted in the chamber too, primping and posing before my astounded parents in a manner I'd never seen before.

"What on earth is our cousin doing?" whispered Eleanora in my ear, brows raised as Eleanor flapped her arms animatedly, her cheeks stained blood-red.

"Showing off, I should think. She's awful, Eleonora—our cousin *Smell*-anor."

Eleanora gave me a rather disapproving look but the corner of her full red mouth quirked upwards. Both Megot and Joanie tried to hide their sniggers, but failing miserably. I saw Father move his head and his piercing, half-hooded eye fixed upon them.

"Stop it!" Frantically, I nudged Margaret with an elbow. "Father will have us all beaten!"

I thought we might be done for, but suddenly Father was distracted—trumpeters ranged around the hall blew fanfares, while the musicians played with gusto and food was carried in for a great feast, just as if we were in a royal castle and not a peaceful priory by a river. Stuffed pigeon abounded, served alongside mince tartlets and crown-shaped venison pies, and there were several plump geese slathered in a rich saffron sauce. Subtleties followed, one fashioned into the image of the priory with a frosted spire wrought from barley sugar, which drew a gasp of admiration from all assembled at the trestle tables.

I hardly cared about the feast though, I was just so glad to see my sisters and Mama and the dear baby. Oh, yes, and Father too, for all his gruffness! Beside me, Joan was talking animatedly of the family's recent adventures—the entire royal entourage had visited the shrine at Glastonbury and then travelled west to Exeter.

"It was wonderful—until I became ill." Eleanora gave a mournful sniff. "The physic says I caught an ague from inhaling the cold Dorset sea-air. Mother says I must eat a special diet for a while due to my frail constitution." She gestured to her trencher—spiced fish to help clear the nose, sweet almonds and dried figs from Spain to aid digestion, lemon sherbet to help soothe a rough throat.

"You will be better soon, I hope." I watched as she delicately dabbed her reddened nose, praying her ague would not afflict me. Nothing was worse than rising for early prayer with a head-cold.

"It's but a trifle, I'm sure," she said. "I'd better feel well soon, for I have brought a new horse and want to ride him soon! I've called him Rougemont after the lovely red castle we stayed in at Exeter!"

"A horse! Where is he?" I squealed. I loved horses…and hounds and hawks.

"The grooms have taken him to the priory stables; I'll show him to you on the morrow. I'd let you ride him on the way to Dover, but it probably is not appropriate."

My face fell.

Eleanora bent closer, silver buttons flashing bright fire in the torchlight. "Say not a word, little sister—but when we are well away from here, we'll see."

I sat at the port of Dover, mounted on Rougement, a beautiful bay gelding with a jagged white blaze and a reddish mane and tail of great thickness and beauty. As she had promised, Eleanora allowed me to ride him when we were far from Amesbury's walls and stern Benedictine rules.

Along Dover's quayside, a great cog draped in flags and pennants bobbed and bashed against the harbour wall as sailors threw down ropes and made it fast prior to the disembarkation of its noble passengers. My sisters stood at my side, a bobbing row of bright flowers, their jewels and golden girdles flashing in the sunlight. Baby Edward, wrapped in white and gold silks, gurgled in the arms of his nurses. Wearing scarlet and blue cloaks and circlets on their brows, Father and Mother stood at the fore of the party, under a canopy that flapped in the brisk wind off the sea.

After what seemed an eternity, down from the ship's deck came the Dowager Queen Eleanor, fresh from her travels in France and Provence. It had been a year or more since I had last seen her but I remembered well her sweet perfume, her graciousness, her love of books and the Arthurian legends—and the great beauty that was still undimmed despite her age.

Clad in a close-waisted green gown and a golden cap, her silver-streaked dark hair hidden under a pearl-threaded linen veil, she still retained her aura of grace and beauty—but I noticed she used a cane to steady herself and that a gauntness clung to her cheeks I had not seen before. Grandmama was now noticeably growing old.

She greeted her son and daughter-in-law, then turned to her grandchildren, inspecting us with a smile of pleasure. At last her warm gaze fell upon me, the odd one out in my funereal black. "Mary," she said, "my dearest little Mary, who will be the companion of my old age in Amesbury. I am so glad the Prioress allowed you to come to Dover." She snapped her fingers and one of her attendants ran over, carrying a small cedar box. "I have something for you. Your Uncle Edmund always enjoyed it when he was young."

The servant flipped the box lid open. Grandmama Eleanor reached in and pulled out a glowing amber stick, a wonderful magic wand that shone in the sunlight. "Barley sugar," she announced. "I am sure you have nothing like it at St Mary's."

"Now," she continued, as I took the stick and secreted it in my sleeve, "I think we should ride together in order to become reacquainted with each other. Indeed, I think we should go for a little stay at court before departing for Amesbury—don't you, Edward?" She glanced over at Father, who raised his brows. "I don't think the Prioress would mind Mary staying with us for a few weeks, do you?"

"Lady Mother, she might well object—but I do not think her possible ire will prevent you from doing as *you* wish in this regard. Yes, Mary can come to court. I will inform Prioress Ida at once—and send her a sweetener." He made a motion with his fingers as if rubbing two coins together.

Filled with gratitude, I smiled at my esteemed grandmother, the Dowager Queen. Gently, wisely, she smiled back at me. "Ah, my little Mary," she murmured. "I must speak the truth—you look so small and lost in your black robes. I hope I have not done ill by asking that you be veiled as my companion. Your mother the Queen was much against it."

"I am happy enough, Grandmama," I said. I'd had much time to contemplate my future. Nuns had some advantages over other women: no fear of forced marriage to an elderly or dissolute lord, no fear of dying in childbirth as so many women did, no sorrow from the deaths of one's children—I thought of Mother, who had lost so many babes, their little coffins carried away to Westminster Abbey while she steeled her soul to ice.

"I am pleased to hear that you are content." Grandmama nodded, looking a little relieved. "How is your cousin Eleanor of Brittany faring at the priory?"

"Gloomily!" I blurted without thinking, then blushed in embarrassment. "Grandmama, forgive me but she is a miserable girl. I suspect she wants to become an abbess one day and believes that abbesses are less holy if they smile. We are as different as chalk and cheese, Eleanor and I."

The Dowager Queen gestured me close. "You know... having spoken to Eleanor in the past, I must agree. So, that means you and I will have to be good friends once we are together at Amesbury, no?"

"Yes!" I said, happy beyond words. "Yes, Grandmama. I have so many things to show you!"

When our month together at court was done, Grandmama Eleanor settled into her new, quiet life at St Mary's Priory. We spent much time together when not at our devotions; she brought out her books of Arthurian tales and read to me of Tristan and Isolde, and Gawain and the Loathly Lady, while Cousin Eleanor, peering over our shoulders in disgust, put her nose in the air and stalked moodily away to the chapel, making a great show of her superior piety.

"I do not know where young Eleanor gets her *demeanour* from," said Grandmama, shaking her head. "It must be from her sire; John of Brittany *did* seem worthy but rather dull. It certainly is not from me, or your Aunt Beatrice..." She sighed. "God forgive me for saying so, but your cousin's about as lively as the *other* Eleanor of Brittany."

"The other Eleanor?" My brows drew together in perplexity. "There's no other Eleanor here; at least none from Brittany."

"I meant the one buried in the old Abbey before the relics of St Melor! She was called Eleanor of Brittany too, and was your Grandfather's cousin..." A cloud swept over the old Queen's face. "She was the daughter of Geoffrey Plantagenet, the middle son of Henry II. Many thought she was the rightful heir to England after her brother Arthur was killed..."

I stared at Grandmama, intrigued by this dead kinswoman—who some thought more a princess than me—and her dead brother, who bore the name of the Forever King. "What happened to Arthur? How did he die?"

Grandmama stared down at her hands, lying folded upon her decorated Psalter. "They say King John murdered him and threw his body in the river to be eaten by the fishes."

A gasp of horror broke from my lips. John was my great-grandfather and I recalled that he was an unpopular King; his barons had revolted against his rule and forced him to sign the Great Charter. But the black-hearted misdeeds of my ancestor had never fallen upon my tender ears ere now….

"I should not have spoken of Lady Eleanor," murmured Grandmama, suddenly distant, clutching the Psalter in a hard grip as if using it for protection. Her knuckles were white. "Yet I cannot forget. I saw her once; Henry invited her to court. She was imprisoned for life, you see…"

"Grandfather imprisoned her?" This tale was getting more sordid with every word. I always thought of Grandfather Henry as a gentle King who preferred building churches and palaces to violence and intrigue.

"No, King John did—but it was in his will that Eleanor remain incarcerated for life. Henry dared not release her but he treated her well; she wanted for nought…"

Except for freedom, I thought dully.

"One time your grandfather even gave her a gold coronet to mark her royalty, but she was past being desirous of such tokens. She wore it awhile at Christ's Mass then gave it as a gift to your father, who was just a little boy at the time."

Together we both sat in silence as a cloud passed outside the window and the candles burnt low. Far away, some of the nuns were singing, their voices ascending like those of angels to the rafters of the church roof.

"Eleanor of Brittany is at peace," Grandmama finally said with firmness, opening to a page in her Psalter, bright with illuminations. "As it says in Corinthians: *For our light and momentary troubles are achieving for us an eternal glory that far outweighs them all. So we fix our eyes not on what is seen, but on what is unseen, since what is seen is temporary, but what is unseen is eternal.*"

Fervently, I crossed myself.

"Let us be of good cheer again," said Grandmama, closing the Psalter once again. "It was a long time ago."

"Yes," I said slowly. "I feel sad for my kinswoman, the dead princess Eleanor—but I nigh laughed when you described Cousin Eleanor as less alive than someone who is actually dead!"

"You must not tell her!" the Dowager Queen said conspiratorially.

"I shan't," I promised and because Grandmama had asked me not to, I would not dare—but oh, how I mightily wished to

Over the next few years, I became even more settled in my life with the Benedictine nuns, even if I was far from the most pious, the most compassionate or the most diligent of the Order. Grandmama Eleanor was good company and we spent much time together in our private quarters away from the other Sisters. In prayer, we told the Prioress but, in our apartments, we kept a pair of hunting dogs—and Grandmama had a canary in a gilded cage that sung ever so sweetly.

However, as time passed, Grandmama's health began to fade at a rapid rate. Griping pains struck her belly with great frequency; she grew thin, the last of her youth fading from her face, although her beautiful dark eyes remained unchanged, despite pain and weariness. Father visited as frequently as his duties allowed, bringing gifts to cheer his mother—and me. He gave me a handsome bed, with sheets of linen and draperies of velvet and twenty ells of cloth from the bishop of Chester. I was so pleased he had not forgotten his daughter—but, deep inside, I wished Mama had journeyed to Amesbury with him.

Frequently she wrote, though, and one day her personal courier brought a missive that struck fear into my heart. *My well-beloved daughter, your mother bids you greetings. I trust you are well and honour your grandmother and the good Prioress. Your lord sire passes word that you are at peace within the enclave of our Amesbury House of Fontrevrault. I deem this good, my daughter, for I would see my children settled. I am unwell, Mary; while the King and I were in Gascony, I caught a double quartan fever. It plagues me still…*

Biting on my lip in consternation, I put the letter down on the stone window-ledge. Quartan fever! That was a fearsome illness, a putrid humour of the body that settled in the spleen and caused shaking and trembling, a mingling of icy sensations and burning pain. Some sufferers who contracted it did not survive.

"Mary, what is it? You are very pale." Grandmama paused at my chamber door, glancing in at me. She always walked with her polished cane now; her steps were small, careful as if she feared she might fall. "Have you had bad news of some sort?" She nodded towards the open letter.

"No…no. It is only the fasting—it is Friday, remember, Grandmama, and it is also…my *time*," I lied. I did not want to trouble the Dowager Queen further; she had her own problems to contend with, the fading of her own strength and health.

"Ah…" The old Queen nodded in understanding and she left me in peace. Once she was gone, I raised my mother's letter to my face and inhaled. For a moment, I was overwhelmed, tearful—it was a silly fancy, no doubt, but I imagined I could smell upon the parchment the imported scent Mama wore, redolent of rose petals and exotic Spanish oranges…

Grandmama Eleanor was a wise woman; clearly, I had not concealed my distress well and she had guessed the truth. She must have had a word with Prioress Ida and then sent to Father after witnessing how affected I was by my mother's letter. A fortnight later, with a serene and smiling face, the Dowager Queen summoned me to her solar. "Mary, a missive has arrived from your father, the King. You are to go to court at Woodstock for the duration of Easter along with the rest of your sisters."

I was struck dumb, a rarity for one who had never followed the 'silence is golden' rule. I did not know whether I wanted to dance, which would have looked ridiculous in my dour robes, or cry tears of joy, which I thought might offend Grandmama or the good sisters of Amesbury.

I hardly glanced back at the priory's flinty walls as my chariot, attended by knights wearing royal livery, escorted me out of Amesbury and away toward Oxfordshire.

Woodstock Palace was my birthplace; when I saw its high outer walls and the pointed, red-roofed towers glowing against the haze of trees in the deer-park, I could have sung with delight—but the chariot driver, the knights and the tiring woman sent to tend to me would not have appreciated it.

Gleaming with golden finials, the great front gate with its twin look-out towers ground open and the chariot rolled up a winding trackway to the enclosed palace courtyard. There I disembarked, staring around at those well-loved walls of my earliest days. Beyond the hall block and the stables I could hear the roars and bellows of caged beasts—Henry I had founded a huge menagerie here long ago, although most of the lions, lynxes, leopards and camels had been removed to the Tower now. Saladin had dwelt at Woodstock once before he was delivered to Langley for the royal children's amusement.

The clerk John Le Poure emerged from the palace to greet me with a courteous bow and I was escorted through labyrinthine halls, some white-washed until they reached heavenly purity and others where murals of saints and Christ and mythical beasts gazed down from plinths, rainbows and foliage, so real one almost expect them to leap to life. Chapels abounded throughout the entire building; there were more than six, and angels limned in gold leaf gazed down from beams and cornices.

Le Poure led me to the Great Hall where my parents sat in splendour on a dais; stars were painted on the ceiling vault while great chunky pillars of dark red stone, carefully shaped and polished, supported the weight of the roof.

I hardly noticed Father; my nervous gaze went straight to Mama. She was clad in deep red, one of her favourite colours, with a coronet of pearls and a veil of translucent silk, but her cheeks looked drained and she sat uncomfortably as if she would rather lie abed.

I wanted to run into her arms but tradition made that impossible. After formal greetings were spoken, a gaggle of Mama's ladies-in-waiting took my hands and guided me to my sleeping quarters, situated next to those of my older sisters. I would share with the youngest, Elizabeth; Joan was set to marry Gilbert de Clare in a few weeks and Margaret was to marry John of Brabant shortly thereafter, so they were accounted as adult women, hence a chamber was separate from mine. Eleanora, although eldest of us all, was still surprisingly unwed; she'd been long slated to marry Alfonso of Aragon, but there were problems and the Pope had forbidden the union. However, having already married Alfonso by proxy, she could not wed elsewhere. Anyway, despite her husbandless state, our age difference was such that she shared a room with Joan and Margaret rather than her youngest sisters.

Elizabeth had grown into a pretty girl with intense blue eyes and deep chestnut curls to her waist. "I am so glad you were allowed to leave the nunnery, Mary!" she said, taking my hands and squeezing them.

"So am I. How you have grown! You were just a tiny thing when I saw you last."

"You've grown too. You are like a lady now!"

"Let's not talk about me; my life is rather uninteresting unless you want to hear how Sister Lettis farted during Mass—How is Mama? She sent me a letter which drove me mad with worrying."

Elizabeth's pert face darkened. "Father has hired the best physicians in the land to look after her. It is the remnants of the quartan fever that plague her—but she is brave and strong! Look how many babies she has borne!"

And look how many of them died, I thought, but said no more, not wishing to mar our joyous reunion with gloomy thoughts. And besides, servants were running into our chamber, carrying a huge wooden tub banded with brass. Hastily they built a tent over it and fastened temporary steps up the side, while another crew of servants huffed up the palace stairs carrying huge buckets of freshly-boiled water that they poured, steaming, into the tub. Others dropped jasmine into the water, while one opened up a wooden casket and produced a sizeable chunk of Castile soap, made from olive oil and imported from Mama's home country of Spain—a hard soap, originally devised by the Moors, which glistened like a small round moon. It was a world away from the mushy grey soaps fashioned from mutton fat, ash and tallow used for our all-too-infrequent ablutions at Amesbury.

A luxuriant bath had been denied me a long time, even in my private quarters at the priory, and I was delighted as the attendants helped me disrobe and step into the soothing, sweet-smelling water. A lady seated herself in a window embrasure and began to strum on a lute, singing of Tristan and Isolde.

I was a princess once more, and all my cares were temporarily lifted.

It seemed strange to attend chapel with my family again—not just my parents and sisters but my brother, the Prince of Wales, no longer a babe but a proper little boy in a fine little tunic and boots. My other siblings stood glistening like jewels in their brightly-hued robes, while I crouched, a stocky black spider, in my wimple and woollen habit. On Wednesday, *Tenebrae*, the prayers of Darkness began. Maundy Thursday followed, with the altars voided of their adornments and strewn with shorn branches to symbolise Christ's whipping before the day of Crucifixion. On the next day, Good Friday, the entire court mourned, sorrowful-faced and weeping; no one in the entirety of Woodstock would touch anything wrought of iron, especially nails—for on that day, long ago, cold iron was driven into the palms and feet of gentle Jesus.

In our private chapel, seen only by each other and the priest, my family crept to the foot of the Rood on hands and knees, even our parents, their royalty abandoned in the sight of the King of Kings. My Father, who knelt to no mortal man, grovelled to merciful yet stern God. Mother, crawling forward on the tiles like a slow slug in her heavy robes of dark mourning-blue, began to rock as she covered her pallid face with her hands and wept harsh, rasping tears. Only one light lit their huddled forms, falling weakly from the solitary Hearse candle standing near the altar, representing how the Light of Christ alone held back eternal shadow from the world…

I shuffled about next to Elizabeth, her face a blanched moon in the dimness. The priest was standing before the King and Queen, reading *The Passion* from the Gospel of John, even as the last solitary light from the Hearse candle began to wane.

As darkness descended, enveloping the royal chapel, my mother sprawled like a dead woman before the altar, her veil shroud-pale over her face. She scarcely seemed to breathe. My heart pounded in fear when I should have been concentrating on the sufferings of Christ. I was glad when at last Mass was over and we could all leave, scurrying out into the unlit palace corridors to spend the rest of the day in our chambers contemplating Holy matters.

"I am so glad I won't have to eat any more fish in a few hours!" Elizabeth chattered gaily, as her attendants brushed out her chestnut hair and tied the back-lacing on her rose-hued taffeta gown. "I am so bored with fish! And the *smell* of it!"

My own stomach was turning at the thought of yet another platter of fish but I thought of my position as a Benedictine and said, hands clasped piously, "It is what we must eat for the sake of the Lord!"

"I know," scowled Elizabeth. "I wasn't saying I *wouldn't* eat it, just that I am hungry for something else like…like a venison pie or candied violets!"

My stomach let out an embarrassingly loud rumble.

"I think you agree with me," smirked Elizabeth, "even if you won't admit it."

I threw up my hands and rolled my eyes. "Very well, I admit it. I'm looking forward to the end of fasting. Not just to slake my own greediness—but I don't think Mama should be fasting this year. She is obviously unwell."

Elizabeth's youthful exuberance faded. "Yes. Father wanted to write to the Pope and ask for an exemption for her, but she would have none of it."

"Have the physicians visited this week?"

"Yes, but they only speak of rest and quietude; I do not think they know what to do next. But Mother is strong; she will recover. You will see! She is coming to the garden this afternoon!"

With Elizabeth dressed and ready, we made our way to the main chapel, joined by our sisters and little brother as we walked through the long corridors. The choir was singing songs of hope and praise as the royal children approached; the priest was beaming in the doorway, the newly-lit candles lighting up the gleaming dome of his hairless head. A Mass of hope was held, the Eucharist returned, and then, blessed and absolved, we were allowed to go—free to eat what we wanted and make merry.

Immediately my sisters and I headed out of the palace to the Great Gate, where we handed many ells of russet cloth and eighty pairs of shoes to the poor gathered from the nearby village.

Once the court had partaken of a hearty meal in the Great Hall, everyone left the confines of Woodstock Palace and traipsed on foot to a section of the deer-park known as Everswell. It was a magical place, with trees rising around it and a series of three doors which could only be accessed by opening three locks leading into the heart of the bower. Inside were sculpted hedges, fruit trees, paths and colonnades surrounding a central area where an ancient well fed a multitude of shining pools. It was here my ancestor King Henry II once kept his favourite mistress, Rosamund Clifford.

"It's such a romantic place, don't you think, Mary?" sighed Elizabeth, traipsing along at my side with her free-flowing hair a-gleam in the sunlight.

She must have been reading too many of Mother's Romances—and had missed the horrible (and likely untrue) gossip that said our own foremother, Eleanor of Aquitaine, had Fair Rosamund poisoned. "You are far too young to speak of such things, Elizabeth," I said gruffly. "And I…I cannot talk of them for I am a nun!"

"Poor Mary, never to know love," sighed Elizabeth.

"Be quiet, girl." Joan drifted up behind Elizabeth and tapped her on the shoulder. "You don't know anything about *anything*, and you're making a fool of yourself. Forget 'love', dear sister; you'll marry whoever will provide a profitable alliance for Father, be he old, an infant in swaddling, pox-scarred or moon-mazed."

"Father's already chosen for me as you know. John of Holland, son of Duke Floris. He's being educated here in England. He's not old, nor is he ugly…although he often is loud and has dirty nails, as most boys do."

Joan's eyes narrowed. "Yes, I suppose you were lucky. You were always favoured, being the youngest. Look at the choice Father made for me. Gilbert de Clare." She spoke the name with contempt.

"But Gilbert sends you gifts; he loves you, Joanie."

"Stop calling me that silly child's name. I am Joan now, a grown up, soon enough to become a wedded wife. Soon to be the property of a man old enough to have fathered me. Well, at least I have one small comfort—if he desires me enough to send rich gifts, maybe he will not beat me or chase harlots."

"Joan," I admonished, ceasing to use her pet-name—at least for now, "please do not spoil this Easter day when we are so seldom together."

Joanie took a deep, gulping breath; I thought she might weep. She was more beautiful than ever, rich with impending womanhood, her eyes sea-green, her hair the vivid Plantagenet red-gold, its curls twisted with tiny blue flowers. "Maybe I should run away, run away to Amesbury to become a nun with you, Mary."

You would not last a day with the cold priory floor tales freezing your knees while you prayed, I thought, but kept my peace. It was no use fighting, nor did I want to fight.

"You will be a great Lady, Joan," I said slowly. "They say Gilbert is like a King in his Welsh domains. That means you would be...."

"Like a Queen..." Her face suddenly softened; she obviously liked that thought, even if not Father's choice of husband. "Hmm, I suppose Gilbert might spend much time away; I could take care of the household and the lands, and supplicants would seek me out in his absence and say, "Oh, Princess Joan, she is a most noble and puissant Lady, known for her good deeds, piety and charity to the poor..."

Up ahead, a green silken canopy fluttered in the breeze; Mama's ladies escorted her to a seat set up beneath its swell. Breathing heavily, she almost fell upon the chair, her movements awkward as an old woman's. A cup-bearer brought wine; I saw her hand shake as she took the goblet.

Suddenly Mother turned and saw me, a little windblown crow in my ebon robes. She whispered to one of her ladies and the woman hurried in my direction. "Her Grace the Queen asks you to attend her, Lady Mary."

Joanie seemed shocked that Mother had requested I sit by her when she had not been asked. I avoided looking at her stunned face as I entered the hallowed area beneath the silk canopy, for I knew dozens of courtiers were watching, waiting for me to make some error of etiquette they could chatter about.

"Sit daughter," said Mama, her once-rich voice strangely flat, faded. So were her eyes—once sparkling brown-gold, they were now dim and dull, pools of muddy water.

I sat beside her on a stool, staring down at my hands. "Mary," she said. "I must ask you—are you well settled in Amesbury?"

I nodded. "As well as is possible, Lady Mother."

"Ah, that is good..." A harsh rush of laboured breath. "I worried; I did not think you were suited for convent life at such a young age."

"It is an honour to serve Christ, Lady Mother. You must not worry about me. And Grandmama is there."

"I am content, then. I want to see my daughters settled..."

Uneasily I glanced over at her; the yellowish face, a droplet of sweat on her brow below her jewelled circlet. It was almost as if Mama implied that she would soon no longer be there for us.

"Mama," I began, no longer the dutiful novice or even the royal princess. Just a daughter filled with concern for her ailing mother…

Loud and strident, a clarion blared across Everswell. Between the rustling hedges marched a procession of gardeners clad in striped tunics and hose. They pushed wheelbarrows decked in crimson ribbons—and these barrows were full of hundreds upon hundreds of eggs. Not normal eggs of white and brown but eggs painted with gold leaf and scenes from the Bible. Gasps and cries of delight came from the watching crowd.

Father, his scarlet cloak swirling around his impressive form, gestured to the brimming wheelbarrows. "Behold! For all those who have attended my Easter court, a gift to remember this day!"

Lords and ladies swarmed across the trimmed lawn, digging into the contents of the wheelbarrows like eager children. Joanie was one of the first there and back; I noted she had greedily taken *two* eggs, one gold, one painted with a scene of the Annunciation. I said nothing, however; we were no longer two bickering children but facing our adult roles, one as a sister of the Order of Fontevrault and one as the wife of a powerful Earl.

Noticing I was still lingering near her side, Mama nodded in my direction. "Why have you not gone to get an egg, Mary? Soon they will all be taken."

"My novitiate will end soon and my final vows be spoken. I fear it would be frowned on to keep earthly possessions, even ones so lovely."

My Father the King overheard my words. "Nonsense! You are still a King's daughter and do not forget it, Mary. You have a decent income, lands and private quarters. Go, I bid you…go forth and get a damned egg!"

I dared not defy my sire's orders—and admittedly, I *wanted* an egg as a keepsake. Trying not to trip on the hem of my austere robe, I ran for the waiting wheelbarrows and picked out a fancy duck's egg painted with an image of Christ seated on a rainbow.

As I returned with it clutched in my hand, Joan, having secreted her pilfered extra egg somewhere in her billowy sleeves, pouted and said, "I like the one you have, Mary. I do not think it appropriate for you to take it to your convent, though."

"Well," I said, admiring my egg, turning it over and over on my palm, "then it is a good thing you are not the prioress, isn't it?"

I strolled away, Joanie glaring at my back. Oh, it was a happy Easter indeed.

A few weeks later I was back in Amesbury—and my family was at my side. An important event regarding the peace and security of the realm was to take place and Father had chosen the priory of St Mary as the place to hold it.

With his marriage to Joan looming on the horizon, Gilbert de Clare was riding in to swear fealty to my brother, Prince Edward, and to Eleanora, who would be heir to the throne should, God forbid, anything happen to Edward.

It was my first close view of de Clare, the man Father had chosen for Joanie. Nervously, I peeked through the cloister arches, the young novices of noble birth who had entered religious life alongside me huddled at my back like a flock of curious blackbirds.

Gilbert was walking down the adjacent corridor, his strides long and purposeful. The infamous red hair bushed out from his head in flaming curls, and on his fine tunic was broidered the de Clare Arms—*Or, with three chevrons gules*. I was expecting a seamed, ogre-ish face—some said his temper was as fiery as his hair—but as his head swung in my direction, I saw a broad and surprisingly pleasant face with a short neat beard of a darker red hue than his locks. I was almost disappointed.

Then he was gone into the body of the church where he would meet Father and swear his oaths to Edward and Eleanora. Now it was my turn to leave my fellows. As the King's daughter,

I alone of the nuns was permitted to witness the occasion of the oath-taking.

Scurrying down the corridor with all the speed I could muster, I made my way to Grandmama Eleanor's apartments, where the royal women were readying themselves for the ceremony. Mother wore yellow silk, which only served to make her look even more wan and ailing, but I said nought; a maidservant was rubbing her cheeks with crushed rose-petals to give them a healthier colour. Elizabeth and Joan were both in blue cloth-of-gold and Margaret wore a striking long-sleeved gown of green taffeta trimmed with lace, but it was Eleanora who, for once, outshone everyone else in the room.

My eldest sister was dressed in queenly fashion in a golden gown trimmed with miniver; around her slender hips shone a golden zone, a girdle wrought by Mama's own private goldsmith. On her high, white brow rested an elaborate headdress dripping with green and red gems and carved with holy symbols.

"Eleanora…you look splendid!" My whisper of awe came out in a noisy rush. Long-legged like Father, my sister towered over all the rest us, her headdress making her seem almost an elegant giantess.

Eleanora smiled weakly at me. Ruling a country was something she clearly hoped never to do. "The crown pinches," she murmured in a little voice.

The royal women were ready for the occasion. Hurrying to the priory church, we took our places in the nave. Eleanora was guided onto a dais by one of the five attending bishops and seated next to young Edward, who wore a coronet and miniver. The Archbishop of Canterbury was present, his mitre tall as a steeple, his jewelled crozier flashing with every movement of his arm. High-ranking lords had gathered around as witnesses, their cloaks resplendent, their brows bound with silver.

Father's gaze was fixed on his future son-in-law. It was not a particularly friendly gaze. In giving Joan to Gilbert, he was buying the fractious Earl's loyalty and he was going to make certain he kept his promises. Gilbert had once been married to the beautiful Alice de Lusignan but the marriage had foundered;

some evil gossips whispered it was because she had consorted with Father when he was a very young man. In any case, their union was annulled, and now Gilbert was disinheriting his own two daughters to marry Joan; his lands would pass to her children by him, should she have any, rather than Alice's girls. I felt a little sad for those anonymous de Clare daughters but such was the way of things. Joan's children would be in the royal succession and she herself was third in line to the throne, which put Gilbert in a most enviable position. King Consort Gilbert. (It did not have a euphonious ring).

"Do you swear…" The Archbishop's voice thundered through the nave of the church.

Gilbert de Clare was kneeling on the tiles, his broad back facing out towards our party, his hands clasped between the small white hands of six-year-old Edward.

"I do swear," the Earl's voice boomed out, a deep baritone, a little coarse, as if used to shouting orders.

Near me, Joanie flinched and gave a delicate little shudder.

Next, up by the altar, it was Eleanora's turn to hear the Earl's solemn oath; Gilbert duly swore it, his flaming head bobbing in the candlelight as he spoke the words. Father looked pleased, his mouth tautened by a grim smile. Mother also seemed satisfied and reaching over, squeezed Joanie's fingers. "Will you not go to your betrothed, Joan? He glances in your direction."

"I…I feel unwell, I must lie down," moaned Joan, face twisted as if about to weep, and beckoning to her ladies, she hurried from the church in a manner that was neither respectful nor particularly discreet.

Mama stared after her, a worried frown crinkling the skin between her tired eyes. Grandmama Eleanor gently touched her arm; they had never been particularly close, but the Dowager was kind to her today. "Girls and their fancies," she said. "Joan will come around. She knows her duty, Leonora."

Later, after Compline, I found myself in the cloister. Night had fallen but no lanterns had yet been lit, so it was uncomfortably dark. Shuffling in my long robes, I was careful not to trip and fall on the large flagstones—several had gapped away where underground tree roots had spread from the garden in the centre of the quadrangle.

Suddenly a large dark figure loomed out of the murk, leaning awkwardly against one of the pillars in the cloister. Certainly not a nun by size and girth.

A man, definitely a man.

I halted, nervous. Whoever he was, he shouldn't be in here. Even the monks who dwelt at Amesbury had long departed for their own dormitory.

Alarmed, I jumped when the stranger began to speak; to my surprise, he intoned words from the Song of Solomon: "*You have captivated my heart, my sister, my bride; you have captivated my heart with one glance of your eyes, with one jewel of your necklace.*"

A squeak of surprise and alarm burst from my lips. He…he surely could not be speaking to me!

The stranger uttered a shocked grunt and pulled out of his slouch. It seemed he was as surprised by my presence as I was by his. And then the light of the moon, popping out from behind a patch of clouds, shone into the cloister, catching on an abundance of wild red hair. *Gilbert…my sister Joan's husband-to-be!*

"My Lord of Gloucester!" I gasped.

"Sister…" Gilbert looked rueful and somewhat embarrassed. "You are my Joan's sister, are you not? I saw you with the others in the church."

"Yes, I am Mary Plantagenet."

"I'd knew Joan had a kinswoman who was given to the Church. I probably saw you once or twice at court, when you were very small. You looked…different then!"

Lurching nervously from one foot to the other, I nodded. Although Gilbert did not seem quite so ominous in person, it would not do well for us to be seen alone together, even though I was not quite twelve and it was hardly likely he would have either a mad passion for me or prove careless for his own reputation, putting his lands and even his life in danger.

"Ah, little Mary, you have seen me at my worst," he muttered. His breath was ale-scented and he slurred his words. "Forgive me, if I frightened you. It is only…I fear for the happiness of my forthcoming marriage to Joan. She will scarcely even glance in my direction! Am I so unsightly to the eye?"

"Mmm…no, of course not," I answered quickly. He wasn't gruesome to my eyes; but being of tender age, I was hardly a judge of such things.

"The words I recited, from the Song of Solomon; that is how Joan has captivated me. One glance from those eyes, beautiful but cruel…and she loves me not. I've sent her silks of the finest blue cloth from Turkey but still she scorns me. Lady Mary, what can I do to make her warm to me?"

I could not say 'grow younger' for that would be inexcusably rude and impossible besides. "Joan is…spoilt," I began slowly, "but she is also eager for her freedom."

"Freedom from what?" Gilbert's face creased in perplexity.

"From Father and Mother, of course! From the rules of the court. She desires her own household…"

"Well, that's what she will be getting! I do not understand, Lady Mary. I will look after her with tender care and see she wants for nought."

Uncomfortable, I licked my dry lips. "I think she, ah, thinks, that she will be treated as a feckless child because you are of…august years…"

"Christ, girl, I am not yet in my dotage!"

I blushed to the roots of my hair. "I did not mean…"

"I know you did not." He shook his head and gave a sad little laugh. "From the mouth of babes! But I am lost, Mary, and fear I have put aside one wife only to have another marriage nigh as unhappy—even if Joan is a king's daughter. God's Teeth, I do not expect the girl to think of me as some Sir Lancelot come to sweep her off her feet; our union is for lands and alliances—but surely it is not too much to expect a little liking or at least the pretence of it!"

I held up my hand. "Sir, I understand your anger and frustration. Often I was frustrated with Joan, too; we fought like cat and dog when we were younger and were often soundly beaten for it by our governesses. Please listen to me; it may help. You mention Sir Lancelot, Arthur's greatest knight—are you familiar with the tale of another of his knights, Sir Gawain?"

"A little…but…" he huffed, "I am a busy man; I do not have time to sit down and read romance books like…like a frivolous damosel."

I wondered if Gilbert could even read or write; many lords did not but had servants to read missives and scribes to dictate to. "Well," I continued, "the tales of King Arthur are great favourites with the Dowager Queen, and with my sisters and myself, including Joan. There is one story about Sir Gawain that may help you win my sister's affection. Gawain and the Loathly Lady."

Bemusedly, Gilbert de Clare quirked an eyebrow.

"I won't burden you with the whole tale, but Gawain was forced to marry a certain Lady Ragnell, who first appeared at court as a hideous toothless hag. However, she lay under a spell, and at night she became young and beautiful and Gawain fell in love with her. She told him she was doomed to spend either day or night as a crone and asked him what he would choose—that she be beautiful during the night for his pleasure alone, or be fair in the day and not have to endure the mockery of the court. Gawain looked at her with solemnity and told her, 'It is not my choice to make, Lady. The choice must be yours.' With those words, the spell on Ragnell was broken and she regained her beauteous appearance—forever. 'You have given me what all women truly want and have done it of your own volition,' she told Sir Gawain. 'You have given me Sovereignty.'"

Gilbert's hazel eyes sparkled in their deep sockets. "So…that is what Joan wants, think you? Sovereignty?"

"I know it, sir. That is not to say you won't be the master of your own house. The tale does not mean that at all. Just give my sister some of the freedom she craves, and I swear she will soon warm to you and be a good wife."

Thoughtfully he stroked his auburn beard. "I will muse on this matter, Lady Mary. I now have renewed hope in my heart that all will be well."

"I must go now, my Lord." I was desperately fearful that I would be missed and a search party sent out.

"You will be at our wedding?"

"If God wills it…and the Prioress lets me!" I crossed myself.

"Farewell then, my Lady." He gave a little bow. "It is not often in my life I have relied on wisdom spoken by a child!"

Bidding the Earl farewell, I fled through the cloister, almost knocking over Sister Infirmarer, who was dealing with a nun with belly gripes, and stumbling into old, half-blind Sister Charitina, who was lighting the lanterns with a palsied paw.

Once back in my private quarters, safe from the Prioress's potential wrath, I flung myself under the coverlet of my lavish bed, feeling rather pleased with myself.

I rather *liked* Gilbert de Clare, which came as a surprise. Now, if only Joanie would begin to feel the same…

The royal entourage set out for Winchester the next day. Upon reaching the city and entering the castle, Joan fell into a foul mood, sulking and casting black looks towards anyone who approached her. The problem was *not* her upcoming marriage, and, it seemed, to everyone's surprise, it hadn't been for some time. The problem was the matter of *two pages*. Yes, pages.

During dinner the evening prior, Joanie had been scrutinising Margaret and Eleanora's households. I spotted her counting furiously on her fingers.

At Winchester, her worst suspicions were confirmed and she exploded in rage. "I am not having it!" she shrieked after evening table, while in the presence of Mother and my other sisters. I thought my ears would burst.

"You *will* marry Gilbert de Clare, Joan," Mama said sternly. "You may as well accept it right now."

Joanie tossed her curling golden-red hair with unbridled arrogance. "This isn't about Gilbert," she snapped. "Yes, I'll marry Gilbert and be a dutiful wife. I have thought deeply about my stature in the world these last weeks. I am no longer a snivelling girl upset because my betrothed is not some handsome young prince. I appreciate Gilbert is a great lord of much power, and as long as he treats me as a lady of quality should be treated, I shall be content enough."

Mama frowned. "Then what is wrong with you? How dare you start shouting like a fishwife in my private quarters!"

Joan's visage turned the hue of a cherry. "It…it is the pages!"

"What pages? What do you speak of, girl?" Mama's own temper was rising; she stabbed her embroidery viciously with the needle.

"My pages…and those of Eleanora and Margaret!" Joanie waved an accusatory hand at her stunned sisters.

"What have they done?" Mother flung her embroidery aside; her ladies-in-waiting gathered it up then fled the chamber.

"*They* haven't done anything…"

"Speak clearly what you mean then, child. I have no time for this mummery."

"Have you not counted them, Lady Mother? No? Well, I can tell you, I have just discovered that Eleanora and Margaret have *two* more pages each than I do! How do you think I feel about that? It is like a stab to my heart! It makes me look like my sisters are greater in the King's esteem than I! Imagine—a second-born daughter thrust down to the level of a child and a nun!"

I winced at her slur and turned away, clutching my breviary to my chest. Why did Joan have to be so blunt of speech? By her words, she seemed to yearn to make me her inferior. Were we not both King's daughters, although on different paths in life?

Mama pursed her lips. "You exaggerate, Joan, as you always have, and you speak most unkindly when Mary is in the room. The matter of the pages is no doubt merely an oversight. You must learn to control your passions."

"I will not let this rest!" Joanie stamped a silk-clad foot.

"I did not realise about the page boys," said Eleanora, ever the peace-maker. "Oh, Joan, if I had known…"

"You would have said nothing; you never say 'boo' to a goose, Eleanora!" Joanie retorted.

Mother was rising from her seat. "Your Father will not be pleased to hear of your behaviour."

"I beg you, Madam, to ask him to rectify this unhappy situation," Joan said. "Then I shall complain no more."

Mama gave her a stare that would have withered grapes on the vine.

"It's not fair," Joan continued to mutter, arms crossed defensively. "I will not know a moment's happiness until my household is made equal to my sisters'."

Mama said nothing in response, but swept from the chamber, her robes swishing on the flagstones.

"Oh Joan, you are a little beast!" Megot shook her head in despair. "I'd have given you some of my pages if I knew you were so upset."

Joan folded her arms crossly. "Margaret, that's not the point. And you, Mary…" she rounded on me, "why were you staring at me in a righteous, priggish manner? You were like a gargoyle peering down from a church tower with your black eyes."

I gulped. "I didn't stare. It was hard not to notice you, as you were screaming like an old beldame!"

"Even now you gaze upon me with that inborn superiority—as you have always done, for unknown reasons! You, a nun who is supposed to be humble. You, who with your lax manner and mocking tongue, are not likely to ever advance to either prioress or abbess!"

Joan was almost eighteen summers; I was not quite twelve. Nonetheless, I stood up to my older sister. "I may have no real vocation as a nun and I may never seek an abbacy, but I *do* know a little of the word of God from the Bible. Proverbs say *it is better to dwell in the wilderness, than with a contentious and an angry woman.* I'd certainly rather be lost in the wilds than stay with you as you are!"

In the corner, Megot began to giggle; after a few seconds, Eleanora, despite trying to hold back, joined her. Their tittering grew louder, became full peals of laughter.

Joan whirled around, wrathful and upset. "You're all my enemies!" she cried and fled from the chamber.

Margaret and Eleanora continued laughing as the sound of Joan's drumming feet receded into the distance.

Joanie got her pages. Father would not discuss the matter with her, regarding her tantrums as a waste of his time—but he sent two spare pages to join her company, a pair of skinny young lads knock-kneed with terror after hearing of their new mistress' fiery temper. At least they did not have to endure her for long—their contract was for only nine days until she was safely wed to Gilbert de Clare.

Father had more on his mind than Joan's demands anyway. He had gathered all the nobles at Winchester for a specific reason. Not only was there to be a grand tournament held, where Margaret's betrothed Jan of Brabant would join the lists, but a great feast would follow, during which the King promised a sight miraculous to behold. Something never seen in England for almost a thousand years.

Jousting held little interest for me, so I spent much of the feast day praying at Saint Swithun's shrine in the great abbey. I even crawled down the Holy Hole, a passage leading under the shrine, so that I could be near the Saint's miraculous bones.

When evening rolled around, I donned a clean woollen robe, sorely wishing I had a few jewels to brighten its plainness, and then headed to the castle's Great Hall in the company of Mama, Eleanora, Elizabeth and little Edward with his nurses.

Winchester was one of my favourite royal castles, mainly because it was so beautiful. The Hall was enormous, leading out to scented herb gardens first devised by Grandmama Eleanor, though with Spanish touches added during Mother's reign. High windows allowed in light of sun and moon, and rows of columns rose like graceful trees. When one drew close to the pillars, one could see little shells trapped within the stone by some strange magic; I would often try to count the shells and always failed.

The King's dais stood at one end of the Hall; behind the throne of estate and canopies of gold loomed a huge wall-painting depicting the Wheel of Fortune. A King holding a sceptre sat perched upon its highest spoke, wearing a crown and bearing a sceptre; at the bottom, another King lay fallen, the Wheel crushing him to dust. Dame Fortuna, fair but fickle, gazed on both with impassive eyes. At the opposite end of the room was a large, painted Mappa Mundi, showing the known world with all manner of strange lands and the even stranger beasts that dwelt in them—the hideous Blemya with its eyes in its chest, a Monopod hopping on one great foot, a dog-headed Cynocephali and a Vegetable Lamb of Tartary.

Today the Hall was even more fair to the eye than usual, garlanded with flowers for the banquet. Cloth of gold draped the walls below the murals, adding a warm golden glow. Candles burnt in huge iron braziers while minstrels strolled up and down, playing on lute and tabor.

Mama took her place at the high table with Father, and I was sent to sit with Elizabeth at one of the nearby tables. As heir, Edward had his own appointed spot, and Eleanora, as heir presumptive, sat beside him with his nurses tucked away behind. Joan, Margaret and their future husbands were seated across from us; they looked exceedingly beautiful in sparkling diadems and gowns of blue and red velvet. Gilbert beamed proudly at Joan, who cast him a cool yet beguiling smile. At least she seemed to be thawing; I suspected the idea of being a countess and having her own say about her household was finally beginning to appeal now that she thought about it. Next to them, Megot's fiancé, tall blonde Jan of Brabant, waved to the maidens on the other tables and blew kisses. A noted jouster, the women of the court sighed over him; Margaret did not look terribly pleased.

The feast commenced with all the splendour Father could muster. Acrobats cavorted and twisted before the high table, tumbling and spinning through the air, their lithe bodies curved into impossible shapes. A gigantic fire-eater wrapped in a bearskin blew great blasts of flame from his mouth, while a troupe of mummers re-enacted the tale of Sir Gawain and the Green Knight.

"Strike off my head if you dare!" the actor playing the Green Knight roared, swinging an axe at steadfast Gawain, who deflected the blow with his pentacle-shield, and then set to hammering the verdant apparition with fierce blows. After much shuffling in the shadows, an ivy-draped human skull meant to be the Green Knight's head was flung high into the air, spinning until it crashed to the floor near the fire-pit.

The Hall erupted in applause.

Father made a gesture to the steward standing on his left. The man went down into the Hall, whispering orders to the servants. Quickly they milled around, extinguishing all the candles—and then the torches bracketed to the walls.

Women giggled at first, but as a bucket of water was thrown over the firepit with an ear-splitting hiss, they fell silent. The entire Hall sat in the dark, not knowing what to expect next. With my father's mercurial temper, it could be a thing of great wonder or some terrible public vengeance on anyone he considered to have opposed or slighted him.

The great wooden doors at the far end of the Hall creaked open. I heard deep, ragged breathing all around; saw one young lord, a dim shape in the gloom, reaching for his sword hilt—but of course, his sheath was empty. No one save the guards was permitted weapons here—unless you counted the knives we used to eat.

Long and mournful, a horn blew. A trumpeter clad in a parti-coloured tunic strode into the Hall. Behind him marched a contingent of men, dark-cowled like monks. On their shoulders, they bore a huge table draped in cloth-of-gold that shimmered faintly in the gloom. They brought it to the centre of the Hall, before Father's dais, gently set it down, then backed away, bowing in reverence. Another company of men followed; these were armoured knights; they held aloft long torches of burning pitch. Holding their brands aloft, they gathered around the shrouded table.

The King got up and strolled over to the table. With a dramatic flourish, he grasped the cloth covering and flung it away into the darkness.

There, in the Great Hall of Winchester Castle, was a round table, just like the one used by King Arthur and his band of warriors long ago. Carved from oak, it had many legs and a thick pillar in the centre for support. The top was striped green and white, and the names of Arthur's knights were painted upon it at regular intervals. Between Lancelot and Gawain's places was the painted figure of King Arthur himself, crowned and wearing regal dalmatic robes—I thought he bore an uncanny resemblance to Father.

The crowds began clapping and cheering. The King lifted a hand for silence. "Today you see the symbol of chivalry renewed in the form of this table, loved by the great Arthur, whose memory will never fade throughout the ages of the world. I exhort you, my faithful subjects, to live according to his code of honour—be brave, fear no enemies, show mercy when it is warranted, harm no women or children, protect virgins and noble ladies, honour your King and God Almighty above all!"

Cheering began again, louder than before. "God save the King!" yelled one man and the chant was taken up; followed by others shouting, "*Arthur, Arthur*!"

Father beckoned to Margaret and Joan and they left their benches and came to sit at the Round Table, glittering in their jewels, every bit as beautiful as the ladies of the Arthurian court. Their betrothed lords followed and sat at their sides. Other great magnates and personal friends of the King and Queen were beckoned forward, and finally Mother herself moved from her seat to take her place.

Father then sat down in front of the image of King Arthur and clapped his hands for silence in the Hall. "In the weeks to come, my daughters Joan of Acre and Margaret of Windsor will wed lords who shall provide great alliances to keep our kingdom strong. Praise them and praise valour, truth and honesty, and God's law that we all must live by to avoid the sufferings of Hell!"

Shouts rose to shake the rafters. "Now," cried the King, "let another course be served and let there be dancing and gaiety! Minstrels, play on, play on! Page, bring the wine! Bring it at once to the new Round Table!"

The crumhorns, symphonia and bagpipes blared; a troubadour began to sing a French love-song in a high warbling voice.

At my side, Elizabeth leaned on her elbow on the table; her governess had joined in a dance and wasn't close enough to chide her for ill-manners. "I do so hope I shall get to sit at the Round Table someday," she murmured dreamily.

"You might," I said, thinking of her future marriage. "Probably before too many years go by."

I sighed. I would have liked to sit at the table too, in the place reserved for Lancelot or Bors or even evil Mordred. But as a Benedictine nun, I doubted that wish would ever come to pass.

After the Great Feast at Winchester, the royal court removed to Westminster for the weddings. No time was available to stitch Joanie a new dress, much to her distress and dismay—so Mama smothered her with jewels to mollify her, a headdress studded with emeralds and rubies as large as pigeon's eggs and a girdle heavy with variegated stones, both constructed by Adam the Goldsmith. She looked every inch a royal princess as she wed Gilbert de Clare in Westminster Abbey.

The subsequent banquet turned into a bit of a fracas, however. The conduits all over town and in the courtyard were pumping out wine, and soon many men were so drunk they could scarcely stand. Their shouting and bellowing drowned out the skilful musicianship of Poveret, who was minstrel to the Marshall of Champagne, and if that was not bad enough, the Sheriff of London, Fulk St Edmund, leapt onto a table to perform a wild, drunken dance. He was a big man and the whole spectacle was unseemly; his hose rolled down, exposing a good portion of his large buttocks. Women began to shriek in mock horror, covering their eyes at the sight of those bouncing, hairy mounds of flesh—and then Fulk put his foot straight through the tabletop and fell, roaring like a wounded bear. He was hauled away, under guard, and ordered to pay full repairs.

For a week Joan was preoccupied with Gilbert—Mother nodded sagely to her ladies; "The wedding night has gone well."

But then, unexpectedly, Joanie was back to her usual tricks. I was reading Psalms with Mama, Megot and Elizabeth, when old Dame Edeline, Joanie's former governess, burst into the chamber and started sobbing piteously.

"Your Grace!" she wailed to Mama. "She's gone, my dear little Joan has gone!"

"Gone?" Mother's face paled. Edeline was carrying on so, one might almost think…

"Have you not heard, your Grace? Woe, that I must bring you evil tidings. Lady Joan and her husband the Earl have taken all their possessions and departed in the early hours of the morning. They've headed to Lord Gilbert's holdings in Glamorgan. Joan did not even say farewell to me!"

"What?" Mama jumped from her stool, flushed and dazed.

"I know; it was so inconsiderate of the chit…"

"No, you mean to say my daughter has left London without a word to any, including her father, the King?"

Tears streaked Edeline's cheeks and she wrung her hands. "All too true, Highness. Oh, what a wicked day!"

Mama shouted to her damosels, who were sewing and playing with their lap-dogs in a window embrasure. "Up! I must go to the King at once! Margaret, Mary, attend me."

"What about me?" Elizabeth jumped up.

"No, you stay here, with the ladies' dogs. The King will wax wroth at this news and I don't want you exposed to his anger."

I took a deep breath; felt sweat creep down the nape of my neck below my wimple. I was not sure I wanted to witness Father's anger either—but Mama needed me to support her.

Swiftly we descended on the King's apartments. As we approached the door to Father's closet and the guards lifted their pikes, we could hear shouting and objects crashing about. Father must have already received word of Joanie's disrespectful audacity.

As we entered the room, we saw him kick a table; the leg buckled as if it were a twig, and the whole thing crashed to the floor, showering bowls, cutlery and fruit. "God's Teeth!" he roared as Mama went towards him, hands outstretched. "Why was I laden with such children? We should have never let Joan stay with your mother, Eleanor—she was far too soft on her. As for that whey-faced harridan, Edeline…"

"I am angry too," said Mama, "but I beg you, Edward, calm yourself. A man of your age…apoplexy…"

"You call me sickly, Madam?" His eyes glowed with fury; he thrust a pointing finger rudely into her face.

She was well-used to his rages. "My lord knows that is not so. I just wish to keep my beloved husband at my side as long as possible. I need him. His people need him."

Father seemed to calm a little, although he began pacing the floor like a caged beast. "What was she thinking? Is there anything inside that pretty head? And Gilbert de Clare? What's he up to? Is he so henpecked by Joan already that he obeys her every whim? Or is he already seeking to betray me?" The King stalked to the window and glared out; beyond, rain was lashing, the sky as dark as his mood. "I would throw them both in the Tower if I could, but it would make me look a tyrant."

"Yes, and, as far as we know, their only sin is extreme rudeness," said Mama. "Nevertheless, there must be a punishment."

"Do you have something in mind, wife?" Father kicked at the fire brazier, showering sparks.

"I do. To show our displeasure, we can confiscate the trousseau we were preparing for Joan. It had dresses and pearls—let us give the gowns to Margaret and the pearls to Eleanora."

"Not much of a punishment," growled Father.

"Oh, it is, Edward," said Mama, "it is for Joan."

Over the next few weeks, the rest of us had little time to think on Joan's foolish behaviour. Margaret's wedding to Jan of Brabant was upon us. It was far more lavish than Joan's nuptials because she was marrying a foreign Duke and the English court had to display all its might and splendour.

Mother had been in touch with Adam the Goldsmith again to fashion, not one but *two* crowns for Margaret—one for the marriage ceremony and a second bearing three hundred emeralds to wear at the wedding banquet. She also received a circlet of gold with a sapphire-studded leopard of England graven upon it as a symbol of her royal House.

The ceremony at Westminster was uneventful, but the banquet afterwards was not. Clad in child's armour, my brother Edward rode in at the head of eighty stout knights with banners unfurled. Uncle Edmund arrived with a hundred knights and sixty beautiful ladies. Much to everyone's surprise, Gilbert de Clare turned up from Wales, bringing another hundred knights and sixty damosels—but Joan was nowhere to be found. Apparently, she was staying at Clerkenwell, not far away, but was 'indisposed.'

The wedding feast of Jan and Margaret stretched long into the night. So many revellers attended, they burst from the hall and out into the streets, where riotous dancing—and drinking—ensued. Hundreds of harpists, lutenists and fiddlers played sweet airs, while actors and acrobats from the Low Countries, France and even Italy entertained the throng.

Once again, I was seated with Elizabeth during the feasting; Edward was also nearby, dressed in a princely little gown. Both he and Elizabeth wore miniature crowns Mama had ordered for the celebration. We were entertained by Calot Jean, a Sicilian dwarf who was the court Fool of Robert, Count of Artois and much favoured by Robert's daughter, Mahault. Calot Jean was the size of a child of four but had a great head of bushy black hair and a curling moustache waxed, oiled and curled into a fantastical shape. He danced in front of us, beat a passing lord with a pig's bladder and told rude jokes that Mama would have never approved of had she known.

At one point, he took a large shiny coin from his purse; it gleamed like gold. "Here, children," he said. "Let us play at Cross and Pile. No prizes, as your noble Sire would have my head, I fear, but good fun for all in this game of challenge."

"I want a go!" cried Edward. "I can win!"

Calot Jean placed the coin on the back of his grizzled brown hand. "What do you say, little prince? Is it Cross or Pile, Night or Day, Heads or Tails?"

Edward was fairly leaping about with excitement. "I say…it will be the Cross. What do *you* say, Master Jean?"

Calot Jean gave a whistle. "Well, I say it shall be the Pile, of course. Let us see."

The Sicilian dwarf flipped the coin. It fell jangling on the table. *Pile.* "Alas, my little lordling, you lose and I win."

"Again!" cried Edward, a little stain of angry red crossing his cheeks. "This time it must surely be the Cross!"

Calot Jean spun the coin again. "Alas, so sorry, you lose again, my small lord. It is the Pile."

Elizabeth began to giggle; our brother cast her an angry glare. I leaned over, fixing Calot Jean with the sternest look an almost-twelve-year-old girl could muster. "Calot Jean, sir," I said, "you toy with us. I saw both sides of your coin as it spun through the air on the last throw. It is marked the same on *both* sides. There is no Cross!"

"You cheated!" yelled Edward. "That is not fair, not fair at all!"

Calot Jean grinned at me, his teeth white pearls against the darkness of his bristling moustache. "You have keen eyes, little nun. I would not wish to play for money against one so astute."

"That could never happen. We don't gamble in the convent," I said primly.

"Ah, pity…for I have a feeling you would be good at it. Maybe when you're at court and away from the old crows of the nunnery, eh? Old crows, caw, caw, caw!" He winked at me, making demented bird noises and flapping his stubby arms, and then he was off, bounding down the centre of one of the trestle tables, stealing baron's hats and waggling his buttocks in their faces when they protested.

"It's still not fair; he cheated! I should have won!" said Edward, pouting.

"Yes," I retorted, "but look, he's left you a gift."

I pointed. Under the rim of the nearby candle gleamed the dwarf's double-sided coin. I picked it up and flicked it to my brother, who caught it easily. "There you go, Ned—you win!"

The celebrations wound down. The marriage was consummated that night but there seemed to be some rumbling about when Margaret would go to Brabant with her new husband, Jan. I did not hear much about the causes of such rumours; Prioress Alice was politely enquiring as to my whereabouts, and hence Mother packed me off to Amesbury in a litter.

When I arrived, I was near asleep on my feet, but Alice, perhaps as a punishment for my long absence, insisted I attend Vespers and Compline and then practice some copying in the library. It was gone midnight when Grandmama Eleanor came to fetch me away to my quarters, where I fell into bed and slept like a rock amidst the cold quilts.

When I awoke, I was almost glad of the quietness of the priory, the twittering of birds in the trees outside, the distant rush of the River Avon.

I had enough of weddings and the courtly life—for now.

Chapter Five

Spring and then summer rolled by at Amesbury. Matins Laud, Prime, Tirce, Sext None, Vespers, Compline, the days went on and on, one much the same as the next.

I did receive some happy tidings. Cousin Eleanor was leaving the priory. She summoned me and Grandmama to the nun's dormitory to tell us her good news, sitting primly on a stone seat with her rosary beads all a-jangle and a smug look on her face.

"I have had a letter from France," she said. "I will be leaving here shortly—for Fontevrault, the burial place of our ancestors, Mary. What a great honour for our family."

"The Abbey of Fontevrault also wanted Mary back in the day," said Grandmama mildly but pointedly, "but her father the King wanted her to remain in England. She is too important to risk her falling into the hands of the French."

Cousin Eleanor looked somewhat startled; an expression of displeasure crossed her face as if she was insulted that no one worried about the French abducting *her*. Well, why would they? She was of royal blood, yes, but her father was a Breton Duke. She was no princess. It was altogether different.

"I believe they wish to train me to become Abbess," she said proudly, after a moment or two of silence. "I will be your superior when that day comes, Mary."

"I am sure you will enjoy your tenure as Abbess…should it ever come…but isn't it a bit prideful, and hence sinful, to imagine the death of the blessed Abbess currently in charge?"

"Oh, you always have something poison-tongued to say!" cried Cousin Eleanor, eyes snapping fury, and with only a brief curtsey to the Dowager Queen, she swept out of the room.

She departed Amesbury the next day, her chariot rolling down the track towards the town. I waved furiously as her entourage vanished into the distance—and I was grinning from ear to ear.

However, any joy I felt was sadly short-lived. My petty, childish bickering with Eleanor was forgotten when, shortly after the first snows of winter had fallen, sprinkling white stars across the priory roof, a small contingent of riders came galloping up to the gatehouse.

When I heard bridles jingling and saw three grave-faced men wearing my father's livery pass under the arch and dismount, I guessed what tidings they would bear even before they had dismounted. After conferring with Prioress Alice, the replacement for Ida who had recently died, they were escorted to my chamber where their leader sank down on one knee. All three men were pale and solemn.

"My Lady Mary," said the man, "I bring ill news from the north. Her exalted Grace, Queen Eleanor, has died at the house of Richard de Weston at Harby."

Tears welled; I let them fall unimpeded. The Dowager Queen, who had entered the chamber as silent as a wraith, put a comforting hand upon my shoulder. "Tell me more, messenger," I gulped. "I must know more. I have been long aware she was unwell but…" My voice failed; I covered my face with my hands.

The messenger swallowed and began the sad tale of my mother's last days. "Their Graces the King and Queen headed to Clipstone in Nottinghamshire to open Parliament. Her Grace was unwell upon the journey; she could travel only a few miles each day. While she was at the Palace of Clipstone, her health deteriorated further and your ladyship's brothers and sisters arrived…"

"Stop!" Puzzled, my heart lurching with a second bolt of pain, I raised a shaking hand. "You tell me my kinfolk were there, while I was not informed? What madness is this? Why did no one send for me?"

The man looked terrified, as if he thought that I might order his execution at any moment for bringing bad news. As if I were my father in a vindictive mood rather than a servant of Our Father in Heaven! "I fear I know not why, my Lady. Forgive me for bringing you distress…"

"Do not mind my distress," I snapped, suddenly imperious as an adult. "Go on."

"When Parliament closed, the King planned to ride for Lincoln with all speed, where he would summon the best physicians to attend the Queen. Alas, he did not reach that fair town. Her Grace was overcome by her illness near Harby and carried on a pallet to de Weston's manor, where in due time, she departed this earth and went to God's light. Fear not, Lady Mary, a priest was there to give her Extreme Unction and bring comfort as she passed."

I wanted to shout, '*Who will comfort me*?' but although I was a child, I was also a princess and a nun, if a rather wilful one. Shouting in the priory was not appropriate, even in the throes of deepest grief.

Gathering myself as best I could, I thanked the messenger with all the courtesy I could muster then dismissed him and his fellows, sending them to the Refectory to partake of a meal after their long ride. When they were gone, I burst into wild, untrammelled sobs and the Dowager Queen comforted me, letting me weep like a little child upon her lap. "Why did the others get to go and see her one last time, and I did not?"

"I do not know, little Mary. Perhaps Prioress Alice thought it unseemly for a young novice to leave her convent on such short notice and fly across England. She is stricter about the movement of nuns outside the priory than Ida, God rest her soul."

"Could Prioress Alice be so cruel even in the face of death? Even when the one to die is the Queen?" I said bitterly.

"Yes, even then. We cannot have all we want in life, Mary. Not always."

But I had nothing I wanted, did I? My eyes narrowed, still blinded by tears. I had not chosen to be a nun, even if I had now accepted my lot. Inwardly, I swore things would change in the future when I was grown. A sister of Fontevrault I might be, but I would not be separated from my family, as if either they—or I—were no longer of the same shared blood. At that happy Easter celebration that seemed a million years ago now, the King had said, "*You are still a King's daughter; do not forget it.*"

I never would. The Prioress would have to learn.

In the early summer of the next year, I took my final vows as a nun of the Benedictine Order. I was twelve years old. Cousin Eleanor had returned from France for the occasion and stood gazing at me from the side of the church, with a supercilious expression, as if she expected me to do something untoward such as ripping off my wimple and trampling on it, like old Queen Matilda, a distant ancestor, once did at Wilton Abbey. Or perhaps she thought when I spoke my vows of eternal chastity and obedience, God would cast down a lightning bolt to smite such an unholy creature.

I tried to ignore her and concentrate on the Divine, as dressed almost in the manner of a bride, wearing a marriage crown upon my brow, I spoke the customary words of the *Ordo Consecratio Virginum.* At the end of the ceremony a wedding band was slipped upon my finger, symbolising my mystical union with Christ.

After my final veiling, I was taken to Sister Infirmarer and there, in the infirmary, she cropped my hair short with a great thick pair of shears. Battling my sorrow, I watched hanks of near-black hair tumble to the flagstones, to be hastily swept up by a waiting novice with a besom. Cold drafts stroked the back of my newly-exposed neck; I was certain I must look like a boy, which I found an unsettling thought.

When the rest of day's rites, prayers, and singing was over, I hastened away on my own to 'pray' in one of the chantry chapels—that is, to sulk over my lost hair.

And that is when I found my grandmother Eleanor collapsed and feverish before the altar, holding her distended belly and scarcely knowing where she was, or who she was. She had left the priory church earlier once my vows were spoken and I had wondered why, but had not been able to go after her due to my appointment with Sister Infirmarer's shears.

Making her as comfortable as I could, thrusting a cushion beneath her head so that it would not lie on the floor, I shrieked for assistance. Prioress Alice, the sub-Prioress and Sister Infirmarer came running, along with many other nuns, and between them, they bore Grandmama's limp form to her bedchamber, where she still slept in a draped bed with the royal arms broidered upon it.

The chamber door slammed shut in my face; I was not invited in while they administered to the former Queen, trying to rouse her with strong-smelling unguents and bleeding her into a small copper bowl to excise evil humours.

I paced the floor outside the chamber for an hour or more, sweat trickling down beneath my uncomfortable robes. I clutched the crucifix I wore; a simple one as befitting a Benedictine nun. I squeezed it so hard, it bit into my palm and drew blood.

Still, the door did not open.

By the time the light outside the priory of St Mary had turned gold and then pallid blue, I was weary enough to drop. Stumbling, I made my way from the Dowager Queen's quarters through the twilit cloister, to the sanctuary of the priory church. Inside, I knelt down and prayed before the statue of the Virgin in a manner I had never prayed before.

I was twelve, not quite a child anymore, yet not a fully-fledged adult. My mother was gone. I could not bear to lose my grandmother too. I did not want to be alone.

Alone. *Alone*. Night-birds sang as they soared through the priory arches and swept away into the dark.

On June 24, St John's Feast, Midsummer's Day, when the peasant folk said the faeries strayed abroad and you could turn yourself invisible with fernseed, Grandmama Eleanor died.

After masses had been said for her immortal soul, I wandered out alone into the fields by the river Avon. Mist coiled from the surface of the warm, stagnant pool; the light was glowing golden over the woods on Wall Hill. On the road beyond, through the haze of elm, alder and birch, the youth of

Amesbury were singing and laughing as they headed up the hill towards the ancient stone ring that stood on the windswept plain above the village. It was on ground owned by the priory but the nuns never went there, for it was a pagan place. I had looked from afar, once, when travelling with Grandmama Eleanor on a quick trip to Marlborough Castle—a gaunt grey shadow in the mist with dark birds wheeling over silent doorways that opened to nothing. "Do not be afraid," Grandmama had said, placing a hand on my arm. "It is not an evil place, no matter what others say. It is the Choir of Ambrosius, built for Uther, the sire of King Arthur."

Tears wet my cheeks at the memory. Those happy talks of heroes and legends would never take place again…

Cloth rustled next to me. Glancing over, I saw Cousin Eleanor, still lingering about Amesbury like the smell of a rancid midden. I suppressed a grimace; at this sad time, I must be mature and deal thoughtfully with my cousin, who was also bereaved.

"What are you doing out here alone?" she asked, and in all fairness to her, there was a trace of gruff sympathy in her voice.

"Just…contemplating," I murmured, "and praying for Grandmama."

Cousin Eleanor nodded toward the line of peasant-folk bustling up the rutted road towards the old stones on the plain. "Not safe for you to be out by yourself with those…those heathens on the move. They might do *anything*…"

"Are you afraid they'd sacrifice me?" I said dryly.

An angry little flush darkened Eleanor's normally whey-pale cheeks. Her fists curled up in a most un-nunly manner. "You know what's wrong with you, Mary? You do not take anything seriously. And that's why you'll never amount to much in the Order!"

I fumed but held my anger. It would be wrong to fling my insufferable cousin into the river on the day Grandmama died. I stalked away without a word, leaving her staring after me, hoping that if any heathen from Amesbury wanted a virgin sacrifice, they would carry off Eleanor…

The rest of the summer was truly horrible. Dark gloom hung over Amesbury priory, brought on by the Dowager Queen's death. It was not just her demise that troubled the Order—it was the disposal of her earthly remains. The nuns could not bury her without permission, for she was a Dowager Queen, but while on his brief visit earlier this year, Father had left no instructions on what to do in the event of her demise. He had been morose and untalkative, grey glinting in his beard and his eyes lined, too heavy-hearted with grief over his Queen's death to envision his mother's so soon after.

Grandmama had expected burial beside old King Henry in Westminster, and it was only right her wish was honoured, for she was not only his consort but had once stood as Regent of England when he fought abroad in Gascony. But the nuns did not even dare transport her body to the monks of Westminster, for her allotted place at Grandfather Henry's feet had been usurped—by my mother. Father had brought Mother's body there and buried her in my grandmother's chosen place.

Prioress Alice had sent word to Father of Grandmama's death but he was away on urgent matters in ever-fractious Scotland and would only say in a letter that he would deal with the matter upon his return. So the elder nuns embalmed Queen Eleanor as well as possible, wrapping her body in many layers of cere cloth and leaving her locked in a cool, closed room on the Priory's northern side.

The sisters did what they could, but in the hot weather, my gorge rose and I would often end up in my apartments retching and crying in the privy, hating Father for his seeming lack of interest in the fate of his mother's remains.

The rest of the world seemed to know that all was not as it should be with the burial. The Abbess of Fontevrault, possibly prompted by Cousin Eleanor, declared the Dowager Queen should be buried in France. Uncle Edmund paraded to London, expecting a hearse to arrive at Westminster and found himself standing alone, surrounded by puzzled monks.

At last, my sire arrived in September accompanied by his household knights, Uncle Edmund, and a horde of bishops and clerics. He looked even older than before, grey as the stones high on the Plain; always a hard man, now there was an unsettling emptiness in him as well. My mother's loss had stolen any vestiges of softness from his heart. His mother's demise so sooner after had taken part of his soul.

Almost at once, I was summoned into his presence. He lounged in a high-backed chair, squires and pages fluttering around him like moths attracted to his kingly flame; I felt small and inconsequential. "Mary, my daughter, do you not have a smile for me?" he asked.

"Your Grace, I have little to smile about," I answered, forward, but uncaring.

"We are in death even as in life. You must learn that, Mary."

"What will happen to Grandmother? Will she be borne to Westminster now for an appropriate funeral?" I could not keep the bitterness from my tone.

He shook his leonine head. "No, I have decided she will be buried here in Amesbury. However, I shall carry her heart in a golden box to the House of the Greyfriars in London."

Aghast, I stared. What had come over him? In youth Father had always been close to Queen Eleanor; at the disastrous battle of Lewes, he had even murderously chased the Londoners in her name, for they had once insulted her by throwing stones and offal at her barge. The Priory of St Mary was a fine house with its connection to Fontevrault, but it had no royal burials of any sort—let alone the tomb of a Queen.

"What…why not Westminster?" My voice came out a dry rasp. I was impudent to ask but the words would not stay inside.

"I have much work planned in the Abbey and space and finances are limited. A golden tomb for your mother, crafted by the famed goldsmith, William Torel—and one for King Henry, my sire."

But nothing for Grandmama, who had been a loyal wife and mother for many long years. I could not understand why he spoke as if she and her final wishes no longer mattered, and dared not ask more, lest my father's 'evil eye' fall upon me, wrathful and burning like a glede. To feel his anger at this time would appal me, shatter my wounded heart even further.

"Once that is all done…" He rubbed his long, thin hands with their calloused knuckles and palms; a swordsman's hands. "Then I must give more thought to the Scots."

"What is happening with the Scots?" I asked unhappily, attempting to change the conversation as it would lead nowhere except to an argument. One I, a female child, could not win.

He laughed; the sound was brittle. "Why would a little nun of tender years want to know?"

He had lost interest in me; I felt it. Something in him, never strong, had withered and died utterly. Maybe it would never bloom again. "Well…my brother Edward was set to marry the Maid of Norway, was he not?"

"Aye, but she died on her way to Scotland—seasickness, they physicians said. There are now so many claimants to Scotland's throne, all eager to kill each other—but I will sort those uncivilised lords out. Oh, yes, it will be done, and England will know great glory in the north. Mayhap Scotland can even be ruled from Westminster…" His mouth drew into an unpleasant smile. It was as if he savoured mayhem of some kind; wrenching the suppurating wound of loss inside him closed even as he anticipated slashing wounds into others.

He rose suddenly, huge, overbearing, his long legs rising up like the boles of tall, strong trees. "We will talk later, before I leave, Mary. I must prepare for the Dowager Queen's interment. Go now."

Head bowed, I went, feeling sad and defeated. I missed Mama more than I could bear and wondered if I would ever even see that golden effigy Father planned or the great crosses he swore would soon mark the places her bier lay on the sad, final journey to London.

In the shadows of the hallway, I let the tears flow. No one noticed; everyone was too busy with the preparations for the upcoming interment.

Except for Uncle Edmund's wife, Blanche of Artois. Blanche had been a Queen once, the wife of Henry of Navarre; it was Grandmama's sister, Marguerite, who had joined her with Edmund. Although their marriage was arranged to unite lands and power, men whispered that they were also besotted with each other; they had three sons, Thomas, Henry and John.

Blanche was a statuesque, slender woman with wheat-coloured hair contained in a jewelled net. She wore a gown of silver and blue, rippling down her form like a flow of water and accentuating her still-slim form. "Child, child, it grieves me to see you weep." She drew me into an alcove away from the throngs crammed into the small priory. "Here, dry your tears." She handed me a broidered kerchief.

"I am being foolish, Lady Blanche…" I began.

"Nonsense." She had a deep rich voice, warm with a thick French accent. "You are twelve. Your blessed mother the Queen has passed; so too the Grandmother who chose you of all the royal children to dwell here with her. It is right that you grieve. I know your suffering. As you may have heard, long ago when I was married to Henry of Navarre, I lost my firstborn son, Theobald. His nurse took him upon the battlements to view his father's arrival at our castle. She became light-headed at such heights; she fainted and my child fell from her arms…over the wall."

I cringed; Blanche's was a nightmarish story. I could hear the pain still raw in her voice as she recounted it.

"Oh, Lady Blanche," I murmured. "I am ashamed; your suffering is surely greater than mine."

"I still pray for little Theo every night and have masses sung and tapers lit upon the anniversary of his death, but the worst of the grief has passed, although the memories remain. So it will be with you eventually, little Mary."

I began to tear up again at her kindness. "I understand my mother and grandmother are now with God, all pains and infirmities banished forever—but what I fear now, Blanche, is that I will be forgotten here, lost to the remainder of my kin. My father the King…he has changed. He did not even summon me to

Clipstone when Mother was in her last illness. I was not even permitted a last farewell. And now this—Grandmama lost, and not even to lie where she wished to lie."

"Men are different to us; they show not their grief in the same way as women. I fear the King is not thinking with clarity, has not been ever since dear Queen Eleanor was gripped by her final illness. A stern warrior your sire may be, but he held one small glimmer of softness—and that was towards his much-lamented wife. Did you know what they would do at Easter?"

I shook my head. "No."

Blanche cleared her throat. "It was probably thought too *mature* for you to witness, but you are now a well-grown girl, nigh old enough for marriage were you not veiled, so I will tell you. On Easter Monday, without fail, the Queen's ladies would trap the King within his bed and not allow him to rise until he paid them a ransom. Only when this was done would he be allowed to visit Eleanor's bedchamber after Lent."

I did not know whether to feel embarrassed or to laugh; it seemed almost impossible my steel-eyed father, greatest warrior of England, would pretend to be a captive of women even in jest. Obviously, there was much about my parents that I had never known.

"I…I am just afraid I will be forgotten in St Mary's, Blanche," I said. "Out of sight, far from Father's mind."

"Then you must constantly remind him, Mary. You can write, can you not?"

"Yes, in Latin, French and English. I have been taught well."

"Ask him if you can go to court on occasion. Enlist the help of your sisters if you must."

"But I am a nun!" I plucked at my coarse black robes. "The final vows have been spoken!"

"You are also a princess, Mary. Never forget that. You are not an ordinary nun."

A little, wobbly smile jerked at my lips. I was a princess. That is what I had claimed all along. Father himself had said it. I was content with my nun-hood, although I had no true vocation—but I was loath to give up all I had been born to. I would remind Father of what he had once told me at Woodstock, should he forget.

I would take great heed of the wise words of Blanche of Artois.

Chapter Six

With both Mother and Grandmama gone, I endeavoured to make sure I stayed high in Father's favour. I wrote to him in earnest begging that he must write back swiftly to tell me all his doings. I thought he might refuse, thinking letters to a child foolish and inconsequential, but to my surprise, on rare occasions letters came. They were not warm and full of sweetness but in some ways, I respected him for speaking his mind to me, despite my youth. In 1293, I was permitted to visit him at court; hastily I gathered five fellow nuns, girls of higher spirits than the average nun, and hurried to Winchester and thence to London. While the other nuns 'oohed' and 'aahed' around Westminster, I dined as a noblewoman with my sire, eating swan, peacock and frumenty in his private quarters.

"You are well, Mary?" he asked while tearing off the leg of a chicken slathered in saffron gravy.

"Very well, sire," I answered, "although, I would wish to travel more. On the business of the priory, of course," I added quickly.

He stroked his beard, stained with the yellow saffron. A servant, noticing, dabbed at it with a fine linen cloth. "Of course, I would expect nothing less of you, Mary. I will send a missive to that old termagant of a Prioress…What's her name, Aline, Adela, was it?"

"Alice, your Grace."

"Oh, yes, Alice. I will suggest you might soon travel beyond the priory to go on pilgrimages and the like, suitably accompanied, as befitting both station and vocation, perhaps with the view to increasing your standing at Amesbury—perhaps even becoming sub-regent of the priory or higher at some time in the future."

I chewed my lip; I wanted this freedom desperately, *but…* "I am still very young. Fourteen, sire. I am not sure Prioress Alice would permit it. She is sterner than her predecessor, Ida."

"You are a King's daughter. You are *my* daughter and so not like the timid womenfolk of lesser men. It is good to start on your life's course at a young age. And stern though the Prioress may be, she will yield to my wishes."

A grin split my face. After the horrible coldness the King had shown at Grandmama Eleanor's entombment, he was finally beginning to thaw out. Occasionally, I even saw the trace of a smile tilt the corner of his stern mouth. "I thank you for your confidence in me, your Grace."

He sighed, leaning back in his seat with his hands folded upon his cloth-of-gold-clad belly. "Your mother did not want you to become a nun, as you know. In memory of her, whom I loved beyond all others, I will at least make your life at Amesbury as pleasant as possible."

"Oh, Lord Father, you don't know how joyous that makes me feel!"

"I can guess; I see it on your face. I will proceed with writing to Alice. After all, I do want you to attend your sister Elizabeth's nuptials when the time comes."

"Oh…Elizabeth is to wed at last?"

"Not quite yet but soon. John of Holland is still the best choice. A decent enough union; it will do England well to have strong allies in the wool trade."

"It will be hard for Elizabeth to fare abroad…" It was strange to think of my youngest sister leaving England. She seemed such a child still, but then Grandmama Eleanor had been only twelve at the time of her marriage to King Henry.

"Yes, at present she is not happy at the thought, but that may change as she matures. If her attitude does *not* change, well…I hope you will be able to talk sense into the girl. You can give her guidance—you've done your duty as a daughter; you'll have to convince Elizabeth of hers!"

I returned to Amesbury and soon, to my joy, gained permission from Alice to go on pilgrimages as the King wished. With my income doubled after my grandmother's demise, I toured St Edmundsbury and Walsingham in style—as a princess should—accompanied by an entourage of twenty or more nuns and servants, all on fine horses, with a pair of hounds running alongside and a gaggle of skilled handlers to keep them in check. I also travelled to Bristol to witness my sister Eleanora's wedding on the Sunday after the Feast of the Holy Rood—finally a husband was found for my eldest sister, who was sore in danger of ending up a childless spinster. Alfonso of Aragon had died some months before, leaving her free to wed at last. Father matched her to Henri of Bar, a stalwart ally but only a count. The marriage was perhaps a bit of a come-down for Eleanora as should young Edward die, she was still heir presumptive to the throne, but if she felt slighted, she made no complaint, being the most biddable and accepting of all of us. I journeyed down to the port city in a chariot with Elizabeth and Edward; Elizabeth had complained bitterly of her own projected marriage the entire way.

"You don't think father will really make me marry that John, will you?" she asked over and over.

"Well, yes, he will. Why do you seem so against the match? You told me you thought he was fine before—save for his dirty nails."

A dark look crossed her features. "I am older. And wiser."

"Look, all will be well. Margaret is married, is she not? Another John…oh, they call him Jan, don't they, as they do in his own country of Brabant."

"She doesn't like him much," Elizabeth said.

"What a wicked thing to say!"

"You don't know anything," said Elizabeth rudely, "shut away in that convent in Amesbury. He dallies with women almost under her nose!"

"Elizabeth!" I gasped. "You are too young to know of such matters!"

"Maybe, but I do. I have seen Megot crying."

"What does Father say?"

She shrugged. "Nothing. He was not faithless in his marriage but then…he's Father. He won't object if his son-in-law has a…a mistress. Half the court's men have them. I *know,* Mary, because I've been at court."

I was shocked to silence. I'd seen Jan's eyes on pretty maidens but thought it was all in harmless fun. That he would not dare do wrong to a King's daughter.

All through Eleanora's beautiful wedding service in St Augustine's Abbey, I could only think of my other poor sister, Margaret—and it made me rather glad I would not experience the like. I only hoped Elizabeth's awareness of Megot's plight would not completely colour her view towards the marriage she had no choice but to make.

Time passed. Word reached England that Floris, the Count of Holland, had been cruelly murdered. Ugly rumours abounded that Father had a hand in his death, even if he had not countenanced his killing—Floris had turned his alliance to France and Father had stopped all trade with Holland. A gang of nobles had been contracted to kidnap Floris and force him to renounce allegiance to the French, but the plot had gone horribly wrong. When surrounded by angry peasants who demanded Floris' release, one of his captors, Gerard of Velzen, panicked and slew the Count before them all.

However, despite this tragedy, the contracted marriage of Elizabeth and John of Holland was still set to go ahead; in fact, it was perhaps even more important now, as Father could impress his ideas for trade agreements and personal alliances upon the young Count. So, on a freezing cold day not long after Christ's Mass in 1296, I set out for Ipswich, where the wedding was set to be held, with my retinue of noble nuns riding around me.

Once at the Augustinian priory of St Peter and St Paul, I was almost immediately commandeered by Father, whose face was thunderous, his eyes snapping with fury. "Mary, make haste, make yourself useful," he barked.

"Y…your Grace, whatever is wrong?" I stammered.

"Elizabeth! She is wailing and weeping and refusing to wed her betrothed. I have already sent Margaret to her, but I fear she's no use. She hates her husband too, the silly little fool. Marriages are not about 'love'." He made a hawking noise as if about to spit in disgust but he did not.

Solemnly I gazed up at him. He had found love with Mother, but clearly, his daughters would never have that option. "I will see what I can do, Lord Father."

A monk took me to Elizabeth's temporary quarters in the priory guesthouse. As I approached, I saw her maidens fly by, red-faced and distressed, wailing that they had been dismissed. They fell instantly silent when they recognised me. A few yards further, I heard sounds of sobbing filled the air. Elizabeth.

"You may go now, Brother," I told the embarrassed-looking monk. "I will deal with this…*problem*."

Without any formal announcement, I strode into my sister's chamber, dark robes swinging with my speed. On the bed my youngest sister lay crumpled, weeping onto her arm. Megot stood over her, trying to soothe her, but her face was wet with tears too.

"Mary!" Megot left Elizabeth and rushed to embrace me. I had not seen her for some time and she looked *aged.* And unhappy. She'd been such a light-hearted girl but now…

"What on earth is going on, Margaret? You can hear Elizabeth's cries throughout the priory. The monks are running about like frightened geese, not knowing what to make of it all. And Father—he seems furious."

Elizabeth raised her head from her arm; her unkempt, tear-dampened hair was stuck to her skin. "I don't want to go to Holland. John is still but a little boy, younger than me and interested in nought but games and hounds. His nails are still filthy, too! Oh, merciful Jesu, I will miss England, I will miss Father."

"It is Father who bids you go," I said firmly. "I know you have grown unduly close to him since Mama passed to God's keeping, but you cannot stay with him forever."

Elizabeth gave a strangled-sounding sob. "I won't go. I am afraid of ending up like poor Megot."

I glanced over at Margaret. "What have you been telling her?"

"The truth!" Megot's voice was uncharacteristically harsh; her hands folded into tight little fists, the knuckles white. "The horrible truth of my own marriage to Jan of Brabant. He is wicked, Mary. He flaunts his many mistresses in front of my face and raises their bastards at court. I know men whisper that I must be barren because I've produced no heir for him—well, it certainly can't be any fault of his, can it?" Her nose wrinkled up. "Father, for all he is the most gracious of Kings, was constant as John cannot be—he is like a pig at the trough where women are concerned; he wishes to devour them all. And that's not all, he has an ailment…an embarrassing ailment!"

My eyes widened. "What ailment is this?"

"He passes stones with his piss," she blurted inelegantly. "When it happens, he screams like a babe! The physicians tell him to modify his diet but he lusts for rich food nigh as much as women…"

I attempted to calm Margaret; I knew servants would be lurking outside the door, listening. "Megot, please, be still. I am sorry your life is unhappy, but your ordeals must not affect Elizabeth. She is too young to be so fearful. She and John of Holland won't even live as man and wife for several years yet; they may come to be great friends in that time—or more. Everything might be fine; look, Joanie married old Gilbert and although he was not her choice, they had four children together,"

"And now he's dead," said Megot, placing her hands on her hips. "She wore him out in the bedchamber, no doubt."

"Megot, what an unseemly thing to say!" I said, horrified. "Especially when poor Joanie is still in mourning."

Margaret smirked. "She's written to me, Mary. She's no longer in mourning, I can assure you. I dare say no more…"

"I'm not going away!" Another plaintive wail filled the chamber, making me turn to Elizabeth instead of pinning down Margaret and finding out the gossip about Joan. Elizabeth was huddled, knees to chest, her nose running as she began another bout of ardent sobbing.

A heavy footfall sounded in the corridor beyond the chamber door. Recognising that hard, determined tread I jumped in alarm. Margaret grew pale, pressing a shaking hand to her mouth. Only Elizabeth continue to snuffle and sob, uncaring who heard.

Our Father, the King of England, the mighty warrior who had subdued the Welsh, stood on the threshold, his towering black shadow stretching over us like a spectre from a fearsome childhood tale.

"Christ's Teeth! You silly little bitch!" he cried, which made us all start, even Elizabeth, for he was not normally given to profanity. "Stop that snivelling at once, Elizabeth. I have had enough of this ridiculous nonsense. The Abbot has complained…complained to me, his King, about the noise coming from his idiot, undutiful daughter!"

"My…my Lord Father." I took a deep swallow. He had sent me as mediator; I would try to help calm both sides. "I beg you, in your kindness as our dear sire, not to wax wrathful toward the Lady Elizabeth. She is of tender age and loves her sole parent dearly, so much that it pains her to have to leave his tender care for foreign lands."

"I know all that!" he roared; a fleck of spittle hit my cheek. "It matters not! I sent you here not to listen to her foolish woes but to tell her in plain speaking that she must obey her father in all things or affront Almighty God! You have failed me, Mary—all my children fail me."

He stalked towards Elizabeth, who had raised her head. Despite her tear-streaked appearance, defiance shone in her eyes. "I won't go, not yet, Father. I…I feel I am too young to leave your household."

"You, a child, tell me how my household should be run?" A red flush climbed up his neck to mottle his wind-scored cheeks.

"In this matter, I do!"

I did not know where Elizabeth got her courage. Margaret's mouth was hanging open. Her defiance was worthy of Joan.

Father made a frustrated noise, and whirling on his heel, snatched my sister's coronet from atop one of her clothing chests, where her damosels were preparing her wedding-gown and jewels. Grasping it in both hands, he tugged at it as if he would tear it in two. The soft gold began to buckle but before it fell to bits, he cast it from him into the burning brazier that stood in one corner of the room. It struck a hefty log and its delicate tines crumpled; jewels popped out and tinkled into the metal tray below the brazier.

Elizabeth gave a cry.

"My children are such disappointments," snarled Father, and he whirled around, cloak swinging, and strode from the chamber.

The oak door slammed behind him with a bang.

Elizabeth eventually made up with Father. He had her coronet repaired; two of the stones were cracked and blackened beyond fixing—he had them replaced with better ones. Perhaps shocked into behaving by our Father's infuriated violence, she married the boy Duke of Holland without further complaint, but she also got her own way—she wrung a promise from Father that she did not have to immediately go overseas. She would join her husband later—but only with Father as her escort.

"I do not know how Elizabeth gets away with it," Margaret said to me, shaking her head.

"She is Father's favourite, is that not clear?" said our brother Edward, who was also attending the wedding. He had grown much since last we met; he was now a sturdy lad of thirteen, with golden curls to his shoulders and a strong chin. "*I* certainly am not—he is always badgering me about my perceived ills and weaknesses."

"He just wants to see you grow up to be a strong King in his own mould," I said.

"Perhaps I do not want to be in his mould," pouted Edward, folding his arms.

"Well, do not let our lord Father hear word of it," said Margaret, waving a stern finger in his direction.

I did not join in with the bickering that ensued. Father had many things on his mind, this I knew. After the argument with Elizabeth, he had called me to his private closet. I thought he would chastise me for not doing more to make Elizabeth biddable.

But he did not.

Looking unusually old and weary, he stretched out his legs before the fire-brazier. "Mary, you, I think, are the most level-headed of my children. You do not fight me every step of the way."

"I try my best, your Grace."

"You listen to me—in a way that reminds me of your mother, God assoil her."

Bowing my head, I crossed myself. "I think of Mama every day, sir, but I am certain you have not called me to you to speak of her. Is there something you wanted to tell me, your Grace?"

"Yes…" He sounded unsure and that startled me, for lack of certainty was not a trait often displayed by my sire.

Waiting, I sat in silence.

"Mary, I will hide it no longer—I have made the decision to wed again. I do not wish to overmuch, but I have only one son…" He spread out his hands, palms upwards, a gesture of despair.

Poor Edward, I thought, thinking of my brother—my dear brother who dwelt happily at Langley with the camel and his other pets, doted on by his favourite nurse, Alice Leygrave, and tutored by the less-than-strict Sir Guy Ferre, an old retired soldier high in Father's favour. He consorted with all manner of ordinary men, from woodcutters to thatchers, and even assisted in their menial tasks.

"What do you think of my plan, daughter?"

Secretly, I was shocked, and a little hurt on my dead mother's behalf, but my more sensible side saw the necessity of my sire's plan. A King should have a Queen; the accession must be assured. It was indeed dangerous to pin his hopes on one son, especially since so many before Edward had died.

"I…I believe it would be for the best," I murmured. "My Lord Father is wise to think of all eventualities. Do you have a bride in mind?"

He nodded. "France has ever been at loggerheads with England. King Phillip has a young sister, Marguerite, who is still unwed. Marrying her might help tie our countries together and keep Gascony where it should be—under my control. I am also considering Phillip's daughter Isabella for Edward—well, I am not *truly* considering it, I am considering ways of pretending that such a union is to my taste until a better one presents itself. If only Edward had wed the Maid of Norway before she expired." He sighed, his shoulders heaving dramatically. "I did have an idea about a Flemish princess, but Phillip, God rot him went mad and took her captive. She died—rather conveniently, I should say."

"Good alliances are always needed," I said, "even though Phillip and his family seem somewhat *unwholesome*."

"Alliances, aye…especially if they help curb the Scottish problem," Father murmured, eyes narrowing. "There will be no more trysts between the Scots and the French if I have any say in the matter." Rising, he began to pace the chamber. "Bloody Scots; you would have thought they'd learnt what I would do after Berwick and Dunbar, after stealing their precious Stone of Scone! But no, they fight on, under that miscreant, William Wallace, and even defeated my forces at Stirling Bridge. I must return to Scotland and deal with them again in a few months. This time the hammer will crash down upon the anvil…and shatter it."

"I wish you did not have to go." I shuddered. The Sack of Berwick had been a bloody affair, and I could not condone pregnant women murdered and merchants being burnt alive, even if they were supporters of our foes. Sometimes I feared for my sire's immortal soul in his fierceness. I also feared for his mortal flesh; he was not as young or spry as he once was, and Wallace was a wicked savage—the Scotsman had fired a church with

English women and children inside and flayed the treasurer Hugh de Cressingham's corpse, fashioning a macabre sword-sheath from his skin…

"Someone needs to tame the miscreants," said Father, casting me a disdainful look. "You are a nun and a woman; you would not understand. So, go now, Mary. Next we meet, I may have a new Queen, if God wills it."

"I will pray that you be successful in all you do, sire." I knelt and kissed his gnarled, sword-callused hand. "God go with you."

"And you, Mary."

I left Ipswich the next day, on a cold grey morn with a vicious wind howling off the North Sea. A huge cloak lined with squirrel hung over my nunly robes; no simple sandals cased my feet, but fine boots lined with rabbit's fur. Hurrying back to land-locked Wiltshire, I turned aside at Salisbury and sought the great abbey at Wilton, where the shrine of St Edith stood in golden splendour, ringed by many votive offerings. There I knelt and prayed, leaving alms and a gilt clasp in the King's name.

It never hurt to get a saint on one's side when there were trials and battles ahead.

Chapter Seven

I soon found out Joanie's secret, as alluded to by Margaret, and the reason she had not attended Elizabeth's nuptials. In fact, the reason was soon known all over England and the topic discussed in every tavern by laughing fishwives and smirking journeymen.

She had married.

In secret.

And, worst of all, her chosen husband was a nobody, a squire in the King's household called Ralph de Monthermer. She had fallen madly in love with him and begged an unwitting Father to knight him, enabling him to talk freely with her, which would not have otherwise been permitted. The relationship swiftly fared onwards, and now Joan was not only married but pregnant.

Father was incandescent with fury. He had planned for Joan to marry Amadeus, the Count of Savoy, that very year, and not only were his plans were ruined, he felt Joanie had brought disgrace on the family. Enraged, he sent his men to seize de Monthermer and throw him into Bristol Castle as a prisoner.

And that's when Joan wrote to me, begging me to intercede with Father. *He speaks of you with great fondness*, she wrote. *I fear he thinks I am not only unruly but a ninny too! Mary, my dearest sister, I have been wicked to you in the past, but you are the only one I can rely on now...*

Father was in Bristol, along with the unhappy prisoner, so I determined to meet Joanie there. As we met at our lodgings, she fell into my arms, weeping in a heartbroken manner. Despite having borne four children to Gilbert and being round with her fifth, she was still comely; her lips red and her hair beneath her veil shining in red-gold braids. "Oh Mary, I am so wretched," she said. "I never thought Father would behave so!"

My eyebrows rose. "Didn't you? You should know him better than that, Joan."

She wiped her red eyes with a kerchief. "I did as I was bid when I was a girl and married Gilbert. I was a dutiful wife till the day he died. In my widowhood, I thought Father would finally let me follow my heart."

"He wanted you for another alliance, I believe. Amadeus."

Her chin tilted up fiercely. "He had no right to assume. I was a widow, and as thus, not compelled to remarry. So it said in the Great Charter of our great grandfather, King John."

Due to her rank, it was a bit more complicated than Joanie made out, but book-learning was never her delight. Marriage she might possibly refuse as a widow, but wedding without the King's permission was something else again. "Yes, Joanie, but come now—did you really think he'd accept a mere squire as a son-in-law?"

"Will you help me?" Tears started again. "I am shamed before all with a babe in my belly and the father locked away, perhaps never to be seen again." She began to sob. "Mary, I am so sorry for being a wretched little prig as a child. I know I don't deserve it but I beg you for aid. You were always clever…"

"The past is the past." I patted her shoulder. "Children do childish things. I will help as best I can, but I cannot promise that I will have any effect on Father's mood. We must sit down together and plan a way to soothe his wrath."

"I will do all you tell me," she said desperately. "Not only is the man I love, the father of my babe, imprisoned—Father has confiscated all my lands!"

She clung to my arm, like a drowning woman. I felt my heart sink.

I sat before Father speaking of calming, trivial niceties such as the weather and the latest happenings in Amesbury—an old nun shuffling off this mortal coil, a cow drowning in the ford. He glanced at me suspiciously as I told him my inconsequential tales.

"Come, daughter, you have not come to chat about some peasant's cow," he snorted, voice heavy with suspicion. "It is something else. You smile too much. It isn't your normal expression."

Immediately I tried to look solemn and pious clasping my hands together and wrapping my jewelled rosary around them. "Sire, I have heard news of the woes that afflict our family. It must not be. We must come together and not break apart over little…things."

His eyes narrowed and flared; I swear they grew red as coals. "You are talking about that trull, Joan, aren't you, and her ridiculous marriage to that nobody? Christ, can you not see how she has shamed me in the eyes of the world? A King's daughter with child by a lowly squire. Pah, the girl has air between her ears; spends too much time gawking in the mirror."

"The damage is done now though, Lord Father." Earnest, I leaned forward. "Forgiveness is a good thing in the eyes of the Lord."

"So is chastity and decency," the King growled.

"True, but I beg you not to forget your own grandchildren are involved. Joan may have sinned but they are blameless in this matter. How will they live if their mother's lands have been seized?"

I made a loud noise as if clearing my throat. From behind the curtain partitioning the room came Joanie's three young daughters, Eleanor, Margaret and Elizabeth, red-headed cherubs in matching white robes. They looked frightened in the presence of their royal grandfather, but I hoped they looked appealing, too.

The King made a gruff noise and clutched his head as if in agony. "You do me wrong, and these children too, to use them so."

I thought furiously what to say next; the littlest girl, Elizabeth, appeared ready to cry. "The Bishop of Durham said…"

"I know what the Bishop said—he's been needling me to forgive Joan for weeks on end! No!" Suddenly a sly expression passed over the King's face. "If Joan wants me to free her squire and allow the marriage to stand, she needs to plead for it herself.

And I know she won't ever do so; she has no heart, just a pretty, empty head."

"I think you malign her, sire. Remember the fracas over the page boys?"

"That was childish folly. If she has true heart, where is she?"

The concealing curtain twitched again. Father gaped as Joan entered the chamber, clad austerely but her swollen belly preceding her. She knelt on the flagstones, cumbersome and breathless, sleeves trailing in the dust. "My Lord Father, my Lord King, I know I have angered you…"

"Yes, you have. What have you to say?"

She glanced up and there was steel in her gaze for perhaps the first time in her life. Not petulance. Steel. Joan had indeed grown up.

"I say only this, my Lord King, that it is not considered disgraceful for a great earl to take a poor woman to wife; neither, on the other hand, is it worthy of blame, or too difficult a thing for a countess to promote the honour of a gallant youth."

"Promoting de Monthermer's honour is one thing; marrying him secretly and getting with child by him quite another," growled Father but I noted an appraising look in his eyes. He was pleased with her straightforward answer, her lack of tears and pleading. Hope sprang in my heart.

Father gave a great sigh and waved a hand at Joan. "Go, and take your daughters with you. They are mere babes; they should not witness this wrangling. I will think on your words."

"You are too kind, my Lord King." Joanie curtseyed hastily and gathering the girls, herded them from the chamber.

Hopefully, I sat forward on my cushioned stool, hands flat on my knees, "Well, Sire? Is there any hope for my fair but foolish sister?"

He pursed his lips. "God's Teeth, you don't even give me a minute, Mary. Yes, yes, I'll release de Monthermer, Goddamn him. The horse is out of the stable, so to speak; Jesu, I was afeared she'd birth the brat before my very seat. I'll have to see about getting her husband a title, as much as it pains me to do so—Joan's little indiscretion needs to be hidden best as possible, and I have heard he'd an able sort."

"Oh, my lord Father, thank you!" Dropping to my knees, I kissed his hand in gratitude.

He pulled his hand away. "I wasn't going to have you and that old nag the Bishop of Durham going on and on at me. Now, begone, child; my head throbs from all this nonsense!"

So Ralph de Monthermer was released from Bristol's dungeons. I stood within the castle bailey, hidden in the shadows of the frowning Keep, as he staggered out of imprisonment into the sunlight, blinking like an owl, white-faced and seemingly in shock that he had been given a reprieve from the King. He was a handsome man, well-made, with curling dark brown hair—I could see what my sister found attractive, although she'd played a dangerous game and almost lost.

And there she was, dressed as a princess in rich robes of summer-blue silk, but with her head covered to show all she was his lawfully-wedded wife, and she went up to him, walking sedately and carefully with her huge belly, and took his hand in hers, speaking too quietly for anyone else to hear her words.

Ralph stared at her as if in shock, and then they just gazed at each other, standing there, hands clasped, in the streaming golden sunlight.

It was just like a scene from one of the Arthurian tales I loved, like Tristan and Isolde or Lancelot and Guinevere.

Pleased with the joyous outcome, I returned promptly to St Mary's, but Joan never forgot how I'd helped her on that occasion. We were no longer feuding childhood rivals; now we were best friends.

When her daughter with Ralph was born, she named her…Mary.

Chapter Eight

The marriage of King Edward and Princess Marguerite of France took place in Canterbury Cathedral. It brought a little happiness into the family but we were all deeply aware death had claimed one of our own—my eldest sister, Eleanora, Countess of Bar, had died the previous August. No one knew what malady had killed her, only that death had come quickly; her body was shipped home for burial in Westminster. Elizabeth had come home too, a widow—her young husband John of Holland had died after ruling his territory for only two years.

Despite his age of sixty, my sire still walked with regal dignity, unbent, his silvered hair gleaming in the sunlight. At his side the Princess Marguerite was a beautiful young creature with long golden-brown hair and small, sculpted features; her family was known for its handsome looks, her brother being nicknamed 'The Fair.' She was only twenty, the same age as me. I wondered how she might feel about marrying a man so much older than she, but she gave no hint of any distress—unlike my sisters when confronted by the prospect of marriages they did not like.

At the following nuptial feast, I was introduced to Father's new bride and we quickly discovered we had a liking for each other's company. She was witty, quick, and interested in all that went on about her, and despite her frail, feminine appearance, she was surprisingly fierce. "I will go with your Father, my dear husband, on his campaigns in Scotland!" she told me. "I swear I will journey with him across bog and moor and battlefield, and will cheer him on in the war against his foes."

I was so relieved that Marguerite seemed a worthy new Queen for Father that I became quite drunk at the banquet, and began playing *passe dix*, a game of three dice, with a couple of young lordlings. Before I knew it, my purse was empty, and I was in debt to one of the cocky young fellows, a ruddy-cheeked youth who wore a tall green hat topped by a red feather.

"I will waive this debt," the youth said gallantly, making a bow with that poison-green hat in hand. "I could not take money from a fair princess, daughter of our mighty sovereign—and even less from a bride of Christ."

Clutching my wine goblet, I leant back on my bench. "No…No…" I slurred. "I won't hear of it! I always pay what I owe…I don't have the money for you now, but I will, I promise, sir."

"Truly?" The young man's beady eyes lit up.

"I swear on the True Cross!" I cried, my voice too loud and attracting unwelcome attention. People were sniggering and pointing at the inebriated royal nun.

It was at that moment I thought of poor dead Eleanora, who should have joined in Father's marriage celebrations with the rest of us, and I burst into noisy tears right there in front of the whole assembly.

My brother Edward saved me from further shame. He was always full of jollity and a lack of decorum, which bothered Father no end. Quick as an eye's blink, he drew the attention from me by yelling for one of his followers to hop up on the table and dance before the company. A spry man wearing great clunky yellow boots sprang onto the table and began to dance like a wild man in the woods, kicking his heels and waving his arms, while Edward and his bright young followers laughed uproariously.

"I'll pay you fifty shillings!" he shouted, waving a goblet in the air and showering wine—while at the same time giving me a sideways glance that told me to hasten away while I could.

Gathering my robes, I muttered a farewell to my gambling partners and vanished into my lodgings in the Bishop's Palace, where I fell snoring amidst my scandalised group of nuns.

The next day I was hauled before Father. Presumably, the wedding night had gone well; he looked content, like a great drowsing lion, as he reclined on his chair. "Well, you were quite the centre of attention last night, weren't you, Mary?"

I flushed deeply. "I was foolish; I beg your forgiveness, Sire."

"No…no, I do not much care what you get up to away from your convent; that is between you and the Prioress. I believe, though…there is a question of this…" He rubbed thumb and forefinger together, indicating coins.

Embarrassed, I nodded. "A harmless game…went a little awry."

"How much?"

I told him; I thought he would roar, the drowsing lion prodded to rage.

Entering the chamber in a rush of brocade, the new Queen Marguerite laid a delicate, perfumed hand on her husband's shoulder and whispered in his ear.

Moments later, he calmed, although his fingers were still tightly gripping the arms of his chair. "My wife has interceded on your behalf—and as a wedding gift, your debt will be paid. But get you to Amesbury as soon as you may so that you won't cause any more trouble!"

Returning to the priory, my gambling exploits in London had become rather famous…or infamous. I saw a few pursed-mouthed glares from older nuns but more often suppressed smiles, and even one or two admiring glances from the young noble girls who had joined the order through familial duty rather than piety. I began to consolidate my own little special band of followers who accompanied me on pilgrimages to various shrines across the land. Nuns who had more to do than pray, we called ourselves, with ribald laughter.

By the next year, the new young Queen had given birth to a healthy boy, my half-brother Thomas. Men laughed about my father's virility, exceptional for a man his age, but the new baby's birth had not been without drama.

Thomas was born at a manor house near Brotherton in Yorkshire. The plan had been for Marguerite to go into confinement at Cawood Castle near York, but whilst sojourning at Pontefract, she had unwisely decided to go hunting one final time before the birth, and the swift riding had brought on the childbirth pangs. She was carried to Brotherton Manor where, for a time, the situation looked grim. In the midst of her travail, however, Marguerite had called on blessed Saint Thomas a Becket to aid her, and to everyone's relief, she was delivered safely of her son. In thanks for the saint's intercession, she called the child Thomas after him.

I sent gifts of silver plate for the new baby and Marguerite wrote back to me, telling of her daily life with Father. She was chatty and amusing, and over the months that followed, our correspondence blossomed into firm friendship.

I journeyed to Woodstock to visit her and the King after Marguerite had given birth to a second boy-child, my half-brother Edmund. Elizabeth was in residence at the palace too; she had accompanied the Queen during her lying-in.

"My, how he screams!" I said, putting my hands over my ears as the nurse brought the swaddled, red-faced infant to meet his sister.

"He has quite a temper," laughed Marguerite, "like his sire, as you know."

"Calm yourself, little one." I stared at the scrunched, angry face. "This howling can do no good for anyone!"

The baby's screaming assailed my ears. I was beginning to feel rather glad I was a nun and had no need to be subjected to such noises on a regular basis. "Oh, his roaring makes my head ache," I blurted rather thoughtlessly.

Marguerite laughed and gestured for the wet-nurse to take the baby away to feed him. "Can I be honest, Mary? I find his crying tiresome too. I am eager to be on the road to see Edward once my strength is fully recovered. I miss him so."

Admiringly, I observed the attractive young Queen. She was tougher than she looked, with her fine features, shining curls and long, slender hands. She had grown so bored during her first pregnancy that she took horse and rode to join Father on campaign in Scotland. He had not known whether to bellow in anger or react with joy—but secretly, I deem, he was pleased. My mother Eleanor had accompanied him on all his important journeys too. And yet…Father had not had Marguerite crowned as Queen.

It was impertinent but my ever-ready tongue began to waggle. "Marguerite…does my Father not speak of your Coronation? You have given him two sons."

She waved a hand and lifted a slim shoulder in a very French shrug. "No. I have seen the accounts; there is no money in the Exchequer to pay for such frivolity. All taxes and other monies must go towards Edward's Scottish endeavours."

"But you are the Queen!"

"Yes, and I will not be more of a Queen if I have a fancy ceremony. It is not as if I don't have my own crown!"

I marvelled at her attitude. I had met few noblewomen like Marguerite. Suddenly, though, her demeanour changed. A worried frown creased her brow. "Mary, have you heard from your brother Edward recently? Elizabeth hasn't and she is concerned."

"I hear from him every now and then. When he remembers."

"I worry for him."

"Why?"

"Gaveston."

One name. *That* name. My heart sank. My brother had, in recent years, befriended a young Gascon called Piers Gaveston who had served my Father. Handsome, urbane, fiercely intelligent and with a biting wit, he had entered Edward's household as a supposed 'good influence.' He turned out to be anything but. It was as if he had ensorcelled Edward; they were closer than brothers. He was a shooting star, and Edward, who was a prince, followed his flame.

"Ah, yes, Piers. It is probably just an infatuation of youth," I murmured, although without much conviction.

Marguerite sighed. "I pray you are correct, Mary, but I do not think so. It is too…intense."

Uneasiness gripped me; I shifted uncomfortably on my seat. Outside the wide-arched window with its *fleur de lys*-painted shutters, a cloud passed over the sun.

"Your father is not pleased with Edward," said Marguerite softly. "There is much strain between them over his behaviour."

“I will write to Edward,” I said, nodding. “He is not a little boy any longer; he must soon see sense, and put away foolish behaviours to do right honour to his sire.”

“If that should happen, I would be greatly pleased,” said Marguerite, her sombre face lightening. “Now, Mary, I know you are a connoisseur of fine wines. Shall I call for the best from the cellars?”

A grin crept over my face, despite my best efforts. “That would be most appreciated, your Grace!”

As the Queen wished, I wrote to my brother. He was quite appreciative of my attention and wrote back missives in which he gushed over his favourite friend, Piers Gaveston. His fawning over the lad was quite tiresome but whenever I tried to speak of other matters, Piers’ name invariably popped up again, and Edward grew cross if I asked him to put his family and responsibility before his companion. Now I could well understand Marguerite’s worry and now she had ceased trying to remonstrate with him in the kindly manner of an older sister—she was too busy enduring the early stages of yet another pregnancy. She was unwell and bedridden much of the time, much to her chagrin.

With Marguerite unavailable, Edward turned to me, inviting me to visit his household at Langley. I never needed to be asked twice when an opportunity for travel presented itself, so I hurriedly left Amesbury with a small contingent and before long found myself entering the well-loved gates of Langley.

Edward was waiting in the courtyard, swinging me down from the back of my horse with his muscled arms as if I was some Innamorata of his and not a Benedictine nun who also happened to be his sister. Of course, on that particular day, I did not look much like a nun. Along the road, I had changed my habit for a simple silk tabard draped over a fitted gown. I wore a headdress like a wedded wife, for I *was* a bride of Christ, after all, but it was not my unusual dour, unflattering wimple. I was a lover of intricate gold-work and frequently purchased it with my regular income; necklets gleamed around my neck and my waist was circled with a golden girdle. I would receive a tongue-lashing and penance if the Prioress had word of my attire, but my nuns knew me well, and St Mary's was far behind us.

"Mary, it seems like ages!" Edward gave me a bear-hug, dragging me off my feet. "How glad am I that you've come! Here, let me show you around so you can reacquaint yourself with Langley."

Bounding with enthusiasm, my brother guided me behind the stables. The dear old camel was still in his pen, shaggy and smelly, spitting and honking in his strange voice; and nearby there was a lion prowling around an iron cage. Yes, a lion.

"What are you going to do with a lion?" I asked, in shock

"Why, take him on progress when I am King!" laughed my tall, golden-haired brother. "Not," he added swiftly, "that such a thing will happen anytime soon. Father is as tough as an old oak."

"Or an old boot," inserted Piers Gaveston, swaggering up behind Edward.

I could not take to Piers, no matter how hard I tried. He was a lean, wiry youth with raven hair that fell in a shining cap a few inches below his chin. His features were sculpted, the cheekbones high—the smiling mouth oddly cruel. Beneath the dark wings of his brows, shone shrewd eyes such a deep blue they almost looked black. Eyes that took in everything around him, assessing.

However, thank goodness, he was not the only young man present in Edward's household; there was also burly Gilbert, Lord of Thomond, nephew of Joan's dead husband, Gilbert Earl of Gloucester, the personable Humphrey de Bohun, and the glum Hugh de Spenser, who I liked not much better than Gaveston—he was surly, and seemed to regard me as a nuisance because I was female and taking Edward away from the masculine pursuits of hawking and hunting. To show, Hugh—and Piers—that I was not some wet ninny who fainted at the sight of blood, I immediately asked Edward if we might go hunting in the nearby park.

He flung up his hands. "My brave sister! A noble nun but she rides and hunts. What do you think, Piers, Humph, Hugh?"

Hugh grunted, non-committal. Humphrey nodded enthusiastically.

Piers, however, gazed at me from beneath long dark lashes nigh as luxuriant as a girl's. "I think she will be ruined if she spends too much time with the likes of us, Edward!"

"I think, sir, it would take far more than the likes of you to ruin me," I retorted, with a fixed smile that was anything but warm.

Edward roared with laughter. "It's your gambling that might ruin you, Mary! Remember the wedding? When you were drunk?"

I gritted my teeth. "I would rather it is forgotten. Let's go hunting instead as I desire."

With the huntsmen circling around us, we went out into the nearby deer-park and by the time the sun slipped into the west, Edward had captured a young buck for the table. I was gloating, for although I had not struck the beast down, I spotted it before any of the party, before the lymers had even smelt it and started their baying.

My success did not go down well with Piers, who barely ate at table. He walked away afterwards with a haughty swagger, and that is exactly what I wanted, for it meant I could have Edward to myself. I chaffed for most of the early part of the evening, for Edward, bereft of Gaveston, called in some harpists and musicians—he loved music—and spent hours listening to sad ballads.

Eventually, however, he was ready to depart the Hall and smiling sweetly, I asked if we might converse in private. He looked surprised but readily agreed, and together we went through the solar to his apartments, decked out in everything a young prince could want.

"You look suddenly serious, Mary." He sat down on a chair carved with lions and stretched out his sturdy, muscled legs on a carpet imported from the east, with rioting swirls that reminded me of entangled serpents. "You are going to lecture me, aren't you?"

"There has been concern for your well-being," I said cautiously.

He made a dismissive sound and ran his fingers through his golden curls in an agitated fashion. "*No one* cares for my well-being," he said, sounding like a sulky child. "Father is always leaning on me about, Piers—he just does not understand. Piers is like my brother…"

He sat back, breathing deeply, and I had to admit—it must have been strange for him to dwell in a family of so many women, with no brothers near in age, and just a pack of lordlings, all hoping for an increase in their estate, eager to be his friends.

"He tries to restrict my income," Edward continued. "Even when I am sending gifts to a French lord we must impress, due to our marriage ties, present and future—Father's union with Marguerite and my own eventual marriage to Princess Isabella." He made a sour face as if the thought of that marriage was somehow abhorrent.

"Who were you 'impressing'?" I asked, keeping my voice neutral.

"Louis of Evreuz, King Philip's half-brother." An impish expression crossed Edward's face. "I wanted to send him fine horses and hounds from Wales but Father would not loan me the money. So I sent Louis a big, trotting palfrey, some bandy-legged harriers who could only catch hares if they were sleeping, and a pack of lazy running-dogs. In the letter I sent to Louis with my 'gift', I told him of the beasts' 'qualities' in exactly the same language, so he knew what inferior stock he was getting!"

Edward burst into laughter, slapping his hand down on his knee in an exaggerated fashion. He was pretending mirth but I could sense the frustration in him. However, I was horrified by what he had done and dreaded to think what might happen if Father heard of it.

"Oh, Edward, I fear you have gone too far," I muttered.

"Nonsense," he sniffed. "I've met Louis; we are on friendly terms. It was a joke. He'll know my words were only written in jest. While the animals were not of the desired standard, they were not *that* inferior."

I sighed. "I beg you do not provoke Father too far. Obey him, Edward; that is what God says we must do. Obey and honour our parents. You must not…*taunt* him with your friendship with Piers, and you must try to live within your means."

"A fine statement from you, Mary—with your huge entourage and gambling debts."

His words stung because they were true, but as the crown prince he had much more to lose than I. "Edward, I do not expect you to break off your friendship or live in rags, do you understand? But you must be careful. I shall be frank—it is not just Father who dislikes Piers. Show some prudence—that is all I ask of you."

He gave me an indulgent smile as if I were a simpleton religious away with the angels. "I will, Mary. I promise."

He was lying, I knew it and he knew it. But what else could I say?

Trouble soon broke out, as I guessed it would. Edward and Gaveston, typical hot-headed young men, decided it would be a grand adventure to poach off the lands of Walter Langton, the Bishop of Lichfield—whom they disliked, for he was Father's treasurer and held the purse-strings. Lately, that purse had remained closed, causing Edward to cease building at Langley—and to stop entertaining most of his feckless young friends.

Edward was summoned to a gathering of the court at Midhurst, to answer to Langton. The Bishop who, true enough, was an unpopular man, waggled his finger at Edward and chided him for the sin of theft. Inclined to rage just as Father, Edward roared back in fury, calling the Bishop many wicked things—a murderer, a witch, a miscreant guilty of simony and parsimony.

In high dudgeon, the Bishop spoke to the King—and he took the Treasurer's side in the matter. Enraged, Father shouted at Edward to leave the court at once, and told him his income would be shorn off until he learnt to act like a prince instead of a fool.

A letter from Edward arrived at Amesbury, detailing his latest escapade; it was messy, rushed, having the hallmarks of being sent out numerous times by his scribe. He was eager to let all his friends and kinsfolk know how hard-done-by he was by Father, and how it was unfair his companions, such as dear 'Perrot' were not allowed to accompany him in his banishment from court:

Mary, my beloved sister, a great evil has befallen your loving brother. When Father learnt what transpired between Bishop Langton and me, he grew so angry he forbade sweet Perrot and his own son and heir to enter his household...and, worse, refused to allow the Exchequer give or loan me money to run my own home. Richard de Bremegrave would not even give me a shipment of wine! I've written to Walter Reynolds—I beg you, tell no one!—to help me out with finances, but in a secretive way so that Langton and the Exchequer do not find out...

"Oh, Edward," I murmured to myself within the privacy of my quarters. "I knew you would not listen. Now you are nigh a pauper instead of a prince!"

Reluctantly, I wrote back to my hot-headed kinsman, *Edward, high and mighty prince and all beloved brother, I grieve to hear of your woes. I would happily invite you to the Priory of St Mary, to abide with me until the storm is over. I must seek permission from Father first, however; I would not make the situation worse for either of us.*

Almost by return courier, another message arrived from Edward; he was now in far higher spirits. Joanie had come to the rescue and sent him her own seal for his personal use. This gave him access to money and goods. Even better, the King was gradually softening towards him and he would not need any help after all, God willing. That meant, alas, he would not be visiting me in September as planned; he had to impress Father by his compliance with his wishes—the King had bidden him stay put at Windsor Castle where his behaviour would be watched.

Sighing, I disposed of Edward's letter in the fire. As much as I loved to travel, there were times it pleased me to dwell far from court. My brother frustrated me, and Father was becoming crotchety and even more ill-tempered and harsh in his decisions. In August, the King had finally dealt with the rebel William Wallace in an act of bloody finality. One of Wallace's own had turned the outlaw in, and after a brief trial, he was dragged through the streets before a howling mob and then hung, drawn and quartered. His hewn quarters were sent to Newcastle and to diverse Scottish towns as a warning; his head graced London Bridge where the gulls and terns stripped it of flesh.

One rebel down did not fill me with much confidence, however; another would wait to fill his boots. I knew the Scottish battles were far from over—and my sire was now an old man, as much as I hated to admit it.

I tried to turn my attention away from Edward and Father's doings. Queen Marguerite was still suffering from sickness and she persuaded me to become guardian to my little half-brothers, Thomas and Edmund, for the latter part of the summer, with the Prioress's permission. This was readily obtained—it did nothing but good for St Mary's to have constant royal patronage. It would be inappropriate to have the boys at Amesbury, however, for royal princes would not be the best companions for nuns deep in contemplation and prayer, so once they had arrived, sweaty from the road, bouncing on their weary nurses' knees, I packed my own goods—my hounds, my hawks—and we removed to the castle of Ludgershall near the town of Andover.

Ludgershall was a small castle much loved by Grandmama during her lifetime. Small but comfortable, it had new privies and renovated chambers hung with imported tapestries. Beyond the substantial earthworks stretched an enclosed pale marked by towering wooden stakes—a breeding ground for rabbits and a hunting ground for hungry dogs. I looked forward to letting my hounds, often bored in their kennels at Amesbury, having full run of the place.

As soon as their initial shyness had worn off, my little brothers were on me, asking questions in the interminable manner of all inquisitive four-and five-year-olds. "Why are you wearing black, Mary?" "Why don't you have a husband, Mary?" "If we catch a rabbit, can I keep it, Mary?" "Can I ride your horse, Mary?"

Then, when questions were done with, and they were satisfied that I was truly a nun, that a rabbit as a pet wouldn't be a good idea and that they both were too small to ride my mare (but they could stroke her nose) they then began to chatter about themselves. "I am going to be a knight!" "I am going to be an earl!" "I will fight and kill all England's enemies!" The latter was boldly stated by five-year-old Thomas, who made a stabbing motion at my head with an invisible sword.

It was going to be an exhausting summer—the boys were certainly more of a handful than Joanie's daughters, Eleanor, Margaret, and Elizabeth de Clare, and Mary and Joanna de Monthermer, who popped in and out of Amesbury for education and training. Joanna, pious and intelligent, was even being groomed for the cloister. In order to keep my sanity, I hired some minstrels as entertainment, and a good-natured fool to amuse the boys. In the evenings, I endeavoured to interest the children in literature—all the books I owned filled with the tales of King Arthur were used to good effect.

Finally, as autumn approached and the leaves on the trees in the park began to turn red and gold, I gathered my brothers and began the long journey to return them to their mother, stopping in the town of Reading with its great abbey, one of the largest and wealthiest in all England. The relics it held were astounding—a gilded cross shipped from Constantinople, a piece of Our Lord's shoe, strands of the Virgin's hair, a fragment of cloth from her bed, Manna from Mount Sinai, and the incorruptible hand of St James, swathed in the original cloth.

The Arm was supposed to be particularly powerful in its sanctity, so I took my youthful brothers into the shrine, giving them money to make offerings to the blessed Saint. Amidst the flickering candles, with murals depicting St James' life adding colour to stark Norman pillars, the little boys reverently placed their offerings on the shrine, where St James's Arm lay in a golden reliquary box which the Abbot had opened so that we might view the withered, brown relic.

Edmund almost ruined the moment when he said, with a child's honesty, his small face wrinkling on the verge of tears. "It's ugly, Mary! I don't like it! I want to go away!"

I leaned down to him, comforting him. "Do not be afraid, Edmund. St James was a very great man, a very holy man, and God has made his Arm…ah, the way it is, incorrupt so that we can venerate it unto the end of days."

"Why is it all withered up? Why did God not make it pretty?"

How could I discuss theology with a frightened child of four summers? "Edmund—just put the money on the Altar as Thomas did. It is not as if St James' hand will leap up and strangle you…"

Edmund looked even more fearful and flung the money onto the shrine. Coins scattered, glittering in the candlelight. I sighed and rolled my eyes. I was not cut out to play the role of 'mother.'

We journeyed on from Reading to London where, at Westminster, the boys were whisked away to their nursery and I was finally free of my responsibilities.

I dined with their mother, Queen Marguerite, in the royal apartments. "How are you, your Grace?" I asked, eyeing the raised belly beneath her soft, damask robes.

"Well enough now," she said, with a twinkle in her eyes, "but since your father is away, I am restless and tired of my environment. The summer has dragged on, and the heat has been unbearable. I am glad my boys were with you in Wiltshire. Plague comes most year to London."

"You should have come to Ludgershall too, Marguerite."

"I had business to attend to in Edward's absence and travelling in the heat would have done me ill, but now I feel stronger again and would fain travel a little before the time comes for my lying-in." She placed her hand against the curve of her stomach. "I pray this infant will be a girl. The midwife thinks the babe will be female by the way it lies. I would sorely like a daughter for company."

"Would you like a travelling companion while you wait for her arrival?" I said hopefully.

Marguerite smiled. "I knew I would not have to ask you, Mary. I would like none better."

Bidding the young princes a fond farewell, the Queen and I hastened to Winchester where we took up residence at the Bishop's Palace. The castle was not far away, but a short time back a dreadful fire had gutted the Royal Apartments and repairs were not quite complete. It had been a dreadful conflagration; Father and Marguerite had lain asleep when the flames leapt up and had to flee in their bedclothes.

Slightly apprehensive, Marguerite walked around her allotted chamber at Wolvesey Palace. "I did not know how I would feel coming back to Winchester after the fire." She rubbed her arms as if suddenly chilled. "I still remember waking with a fright, choking on black smoke and hearing my damosels screaming in terror. I fled near-naked in my kirtle, stumbling in the smoke and the gloom, not knowing if Edward was alive or dead…"

I handed her a goblet of wine, which she had put aside on the dresser and forgotten. I hoped it would calm her. "Do not think on that dreadful night, your Grace. Such evil memories might affect the beauty of your child."

Marguerite took the goblet, sipped from it slowly. "You speak sense, Mary, but I still cannot believe the King and I escaped with no harm. The apartments are so ruinous that they must be completely built anew. God was looking over us that night."

"No doubt He was. Now, your Grace, shall I call your ladies to fix your hair? The Bishop of Winchester is eager to hold audience with you. No doubt he wants to ask for something, probably of a monetary nature. These men of God are all the same."

"Lady Mary!" Marguerite admonished, but her eyes laughed.

We stayed in Winchester but a short while, for time would soon catch the Queen up—her belly was growing daily. We journeyed about the shires, heading as far north as Doncaster, where we stopped at the famous Shrine of the Virgin Mary. Then we turned back south into the depths of Sherwood Forest, riding to Clipstone Lodge, where my mother, Queen Eleanor, had died.

The lodge looked bleak beneath the winter-bitten trees; Father had not visited since Mama's demise and had invested no money in it. A tile was missing from the roof; the surrounding fence of stakes was green and leaning. Piles of mouldering yellow leaves lay heaped against the outer wall, sad and wet, glistening in the dull blue light of a late afternoon.

I reined in my horse, staring. The sorrows of the past rose in my heart: the harsh fact that I, alone of my mother's children, was unable to see her before she went to God's arms.

Warmly arrayed in soft grey rabbit furs, her silken veils fluttering in the sharp winter wind, Marguerite placed a hand on my arm. "Perhaps it was wrong to come here. Maybe we should make haste and see if we can reach St Mary's at Newstead or Rufford Abbey; if the light holds, we might even get to Nottingham Castle ere it's too late."

I shook my head. "No, your Grace. The woods have outlaws in them, as you must have heard. It isn't safe, especially in your condition. We will stay at Clipstone for the night. It is something I must do, no matter how my heart is pained."

We entered the unkempt courtyard, muddy and filled with ramshackle pens containing thin goats and mud-caked pigs. The servants were few, sullen-faced, even surly; our party dismounted, and with bad graces, the oafish ostlers led the horses to the stables, while an ancient crone escorted us into the Lodge.

A fire was burning, thank goodness, for Marguerite was beginning to shiver despite her heavy robes. Disconsolate, I walked through the hall, trying to envision Mama's last days there. The servants had stripped the walls of their tapestries and the dais was empty of its ceremonial chairs and canopies. My feet clicked on the cold tiles, which appeared to need an thorough scrub.

I shot a hard-eyed glance towards the sullen household staff lurking in the shadows, their hands busy with anything but brooms or buckets. "The state of this house is not acceptable!" I spoke as the King's daughter then, not as a meek and timid nun. "I want the fire stoked and a scullion to brush the stale reeds from the floor. I trust the chambers where her Grace and I are to stay are better cared for than this—and if they are not, clean them at once!"

A couple of scruffy maids in dirty linen headdresses gave low curtseys and raced from the chamber.

"Now...*food.* What is in the pantry? Is there a head cook here?"

"Off sick," said a grimy yokel, picking at his nose. "A griping of the bowels."

"My Lady...you will call me, *My Lady*. So, you were informed days ago that Her Grace the Queen was coming, and your cook was sick, but you made no other plans?" My voice was rising; I felt the famed Plantagenet rage leaping in me like flames.

"We've sent to St Mary's at Newstead!" squeaked a woman. "One of the brothers has agreed to be our cook till Alf is healed. But he's late arriving...my Lady."

"I am appalled," I said. "Is there no steward to manage the household?"

"Old Brian died, my Lady, last winter."

Marguerite beckoned to me. "It does not matter, Mary. Edward has not bothered with Clipstone since your mother's death. It holds evil memories for him. We shan't stay long, just a night or two."

I gazed into her face; she was paler than usual, the blue eyes weary. "You must rest," I insisted. "I will go with you to your apartments and see they are suitable. And when this cooking monk arrives, I will see that decent food is brought to you."

Escorting Marguerite to the royal apartments, I made her comfortable as best I could then left her to the care of her ladies-in-waiting. Then, in a flurry of robes, I stalked away to make sure my instructions to the household would be obeyed. It was not what I expected after a long day's travel and I was furious—and exhausted. I ended up in the Great Chapel, one of three chapels within the complex. It was freezing cold, but someone had lit several tapers near the altar. A faint light shone through the glazed windows and lit the colourful wall-paintings of St Christopher and St George.

Beneath my feet, blue and rose tiles swirled, representing the purity of the Virgin Mary, perhaps laid in my Grandfather's reign, for he and Grandmama Eleanor loved such plays of colour and texture. Of a whim, I knelt and swept my hand across the tiled surface. To think, Mama had likely stood here, prayed here, in her final days upon the earth. Did she think of me, her one missing child, or did she only think of her fate? Was she fearful of death or resigned, knowing she would soon see the wondrous face of God?

Tears dampened my eyes. How I wished I could have seen her one more time!

I stood, shivering. Air brushed my cheek; it was almost like the touch of a spectral hand, almost like she was there beside me—although I knew it was sinful to have such fancies, for she was in heaven, not an earthbound ghost. And yet…

I reached to her, my outstretched hand shaking, fingers clawing empty air. "Mama, it's Mary, your Mary. Can you hear me?"

The chapel door opened behind me. It was the Queen. I spun around, stumbling and embarrassed. "Forgive me, you must think I am mad," I mumbled, hanging my head.

"No, I understand," said Marguerite, "as I understand when your father sorrows for his first Queen. He said he would always love her."

"But he now has you..." Red-faced, I shook my head.

"I am what I am—the second. He cares for me and I for him, despite the difference in our ages. And, Mary, if this child beneath my belt is indeed a girl, the King and I plan to call her Eleanor. After your mother."

We travelled back to Winchester where my sister Elizabeth joined us at the castle. New temporary quarters had been devised, so we no longer had to dwell with the Bishop at Wolvesey.

Elizabeth had not long given birth to a new baby with her second husband, Edward's former companion Humphrey de Bohun, and her appearance was rather weak and wan. She had lost two children already, and it was evident she feared for the latest one too. My other sisters had been fortunate in having lots of strong, healthy children; Elizabeth not so much.

She had also not been lucky in her dead husband, John Duke of Holland. She was entitled to a large dower, but the Count of Hainault found every excuse possible to retain it.

It was money she wanted to talk about rather than her newest child, left behind at her castle with its nurses, almost as if she feared to mention the babe, lest it died. "I do not know what to do, Mary," she murmured. "I have wasted so much money sending my clerks to Holland to inquire about my dower. Humphrey and I cannot afford to spend such amounts—and yet we cannot afford not to try, either."

"I am sorry it has not gone well for you." With a hint of shame, I thought of my easy life at Amesbury, with hawks and hounds in abundance, tuns of wine, and my debts paid for me. "I am sure ...Well, maybe Father will help out. He would not gladly see any of his children in dire straits."

"I am not so sure. What about our brother? His finances stripped to nought."

"He was imprudent, as you know, Elizabeth, and angered the King. You have done no wrong. Ask Marguerite to talk to Father; he listens to her."

"Do you think she would intercede?"

"Yes, she likes you greatly, Elizabeth. She always has. That's why she summoned you hence for the birthing of the child."

I do not know if Elizabeth managed to ask the Queen to plead her case with Father…but I soon learnt that he had decided to waive a fee of £4000 connected with the death of Humphrey de Bohun's father.

However, Elizabeth and Humphrey's finances were not the greatest concern of the royal family.

After a difficult travail, Queen Marguerite gave birth to her longed-for girl-child. The baby was baptised Eleanor after Mother, as Marguerite had said she would be.

But the child was sickly. A priest was summoned.

Yet baby Eleanor did not die but lingered on, listless in her cradle. I could only think of the tales Father told of his lost sister, little Katherine, who had been of great beauty but mute and deaf. When she'd died, Grandsire Henry and Grandmama Eleanor had fallen into such despair the physicians feared for their very lives. A little tomb, covered in silver, stood over Katherine's bones in Westminster Abbey…

The Queen came to me, desperate, her eyes sunken in their sockets. "I fear…I fear that my little daughter will not thrive. That she will not live."

"It is in God's hands," I said lamely.

"And that's where I want her to be—not only in God's hands but in God's House. The evil humours that hang about this city concern me; the air is rank, the winters bitter, the summers muggy and full of plague. Please, Mary, when she is a little older and stronger, will you take your little sister to be raised by the nuns—and by yourself?"

My mouth dropped open. Over the past few years, yes, I had helped educate Joanie's daughters from both marriages. I expected Elizabeth would also send her daughters to Amesbury if, God willing, some of her children lived past babyhood. But a sickly child…

I could not say no. Marguerite was my friend—and my Queen. The new baby was my half-sister. "It will have to be when she is weaned from the wetnurse's teat," I warned. "Amesbury is not equipped to deal with small infants."

"Yes, yes, of course," Marguerite nodded. Relief flooded her fatigued visage.

"I will also need to have permission granted by the new Prioress, Joan de Genes—although I do not see that being a problem."

That evening I wrote to Prioress Joan, and as I expected, gained the necessary permission for the arrival of the baby princess from both Joan and Cousin Eleanor, who was now, as she had always desired, lording it over other nuns as the Holy Reverend Abbess of Fontevrault. Once the little girl arrived, the Priory of St Mary's of Amesbury would never be the same again.

But I was not going back to Amesbury. Not yet. Marguerite bid me stay at her side for a while, as trouble was brewing.

Chapter Nine

Father was ill and Scotland was a tinderbox ready to ignite. The year before, the King had executed the troublesome William Wallace—a grotesque spectacle in which Wallace was dragged through the streets, hanged by the neck, disembowelled before his very eyes, and his entrails cast into a fire while he still lived. The final beheading was a mercy. In the wake of his death, the Scottish lords fell silent for a brief time, but in February, one of the contenders for the Scottish throne, Robert the Bruce, Earl of Carrick, mercilessly slew another contender, John Comyn, while they spoke within a church and claimed the crown of Scotland for himself. Despite some outrage over Comyn's murder, many Scots flocked to the Bruce's banner, and the borders burned again.

The King wanted to ride north as soon as possible but, while staying at Winchester with Marguerite, a sudden illness fell upon him. Bedridden, he could hardly walk a few paces, let alone ride in armour.

Having finally made peace with my brother Edward over his misdeeds and fecklessness, he proposed sending him to Scotland with a large contingent of men. Eyes crackling, daring any to gainsay him, he muttered, "Perhaps it is time that my son and heir learns the ways of war. I myself will follow on to join my army if God permits."

Alas, the Good Lord did *not* send some supernatural might to aid my father and he ended up travelling to London in a litter instead. Marguerite was beside herself with worry, both for her ailing husband and the fragile little daughter who grizzled fitfully in her cradle.

I rode on my palfrey alongside Father's litter, watching his liverish, sweat-washed face poke through the hangings on the litter every now and then. "Blast these aching bones!" he snarled. "Travelling in this…this *thing,* like a woman or a corpse on a pall! It makes me wroth that my body has failed me so and will not obey my commands!"

"You must rest, Father," I murmured. "Your physicians say that rest is essential for your health."

"Don't patronise me, daughter!" he snapped back, eyes dark and furious, teeth clamped together so that his words were near growls. "I am not in my dotage and will not be treated as if I am."

"You wound me, sir!"

"I bloody well will if you don't stop!"

"I am not your enemy, sire. I am ever your dutiful daughter, but like the Queen, I fear for you."

He flushed purple and I thought to hear the old Leopard of England roar like an embattled Lion but suddenly an expression I'd never seen before—resignation—crossed his features and he flopped limply back onto his cushions. "Pah! I am like a briar, full of thorns."

"It has always been your way, my lord Father." I suppressed a smile.

"Impertinent again."

"Yes, I am, I do not deny it."

The King leaned on his elbow, observing me with slit eyes. "Perhaps…perhaps you are right. Perhaps I should rest more."

I grasped my saddle to keep from falling off my steed.

"Most of my trusted men are dead. Only Henry de Lacy remains—oh, and Bigod too, Roger Bigod, but he is ill and not likely to live much longer. Perhaps it is time…no, I can pretend no longer, it *is* time to make knights anew from the younger generation, to inspire new young men to fight for England's glory! It is time Edward was knighted; it might give him some responsibility—and I'll need to see about his wedding to Isabella of France. That should give him something to think about, besides Gaveston." His face filled with revulsion as he spoke the Gascon's name.

"Isabella is just a child," I reminded him.

"Aye, but she won't be for long, and they say she's beautiful to look upon. She was not my first choice for Edward, as you know, but she might be useful yet."

A cloud suddenly slipped over the sun and I shivered; I was not sure why. Perhaps I felt a little apprehensive and a little worried for the child who would come from France to wed my often-thoughtless brother. To turn him from his favourite—was Father expecting too much from a naive girl? I had heard the darker rumours about my brother's 'friendship' with Piers, although I did not fully believe them—Edward, after all, had a bastard-born son, Adam FitzRoy, whom he sent coin to for his keep.

Father was murmuring to himself in the confines of his hated litter, obviously no longer interested in conversion with a nun. In his mind, he was mulling over the next steps—steps to build up a loyal and formidable new band of allies. "The young men will come to London—all of them, anyone whose father was at least a knight. At Whitsun, they will come to form the greatest company of knights ever known…and they will vow to subdue our bitterest enemies, the Scots, at a Feast of Swans!"

Raising his head, he cleared his throat, his attention on me once more. "There will be more weddings, Mary. I suppose you, as a woman, will like that."

My brows lifted a little but I kept my face neutral. "Who, your Grace?"

"Eleanora's child, Joanna of Bar. Young for marriage as men account it, but with both her parents dead, marrying her off is the best course of action."

I crossed myself and hung my head. Poor Eleanora. We had never found out what killed her, she was only thirty-nine summers old. Perhaps it was worry and grief—her husband Henri was languishing in prison at the time. Later, he went to fight the Holy Roman Emperor in Cyprus and took wounds from which he never recovered, leaving his young daughter an orphan. I had seen young Joanna at Winchester but had not realised she was already earmarked for marriage.

"I have chosen John de Warenne for her husband. The young Earl of Surrey. I am sure he will be more than suitable. Elizabeth de Clare will be the other bride; I have chosen Hugh de Spenser for her."

I was silent. I did not know de Warenne, but Hugh! I recalled the spotty, sulky lad who had tailed my brother and Gaveston at Langley. An opinionated boy with a manipulative streak. Of course, he was older now and perhaps had matured. How strange all these changes seemed; how remorselessly the years were flying by! For me, life went on much the same, but for my kin…

London was heaving with crowds when the royal entourage arrived. Over three hundred youths had come to be knighted and the city inns overflowed. Temporary shelters were placed in the courtyard of the Knights Templar, where the Brothers had torn out fruit trees and demolished walls to make room for the newcomers. Street conduits flowed with wine and banners fluttered over the city walls. Lanes and streets were full of pedlars, merchants, thieves, pie-men, ribbon-sellers, harlots in scarlet wigs, ladies' litters, mounted soldiers, knights sporting all manner of devices, camelots selling dubious relics, apothecaries tempting onlookers with cures for toothache, belly-ache and noxious fluxes.

I was glad to reach Westminster; the press was thickest around the royal escort and it was strange and uncomfortable to be scrutinised by so many people. Soldiers had to thrust spears into the crowd to keep the onlookers from getting too close, which elicited a stream of curses and the occasional scuffle.

Once behind closed doors, I did not have much time to recover from my journey, however. Joanna of Bar's marriage ceremony was to take place in the Abbey and as her aunt, I was expected to attend. Dusting down my robes, washing my face to give me vibrancy after my hours on the dusty road, I met with my sisters Joan and Elizabeth and together we entered the great Abbey, where generations of my ancestors lay in their final slumber. I passed Mama's tomb, gleaming gold, covered in shields bearing the Arms of England, Castile and Ponthieu; I passed Eleanora's modest tomb, deep in a chantry chapel, I passed the fine effigy of Grandfather Henry, which, if wishes had been honoured, should have lain near to one for Grandmama Eleanor. I thought of the poignant drawing scratched out on the inside of Henry's coffin-lid, lying before his sightless eyes for eternity—his Queen, veiled and in prayer, and his granddaughter dressed in nun's robes.

For a moment, tears dampened my eyes as I remembered the Dowager and the innocent child I was when I first accompanied her at Amesbury, but then my attention was drawn to the scene in the Abbey nave. The high altar stood ringed by candle-light, a cloth of gold glimmering upon it; the Rood a mass of blood-red garnets and other precious gems. The King and Queen had taken their places, wearing their crowns and clad in robes of ermine.

Little Joanna of Bar stepped forward. She was what? Ten summers old? Small and thin, pale hair framed a long oval face. She was too young for her marriage to be consummated; hence she would dwell with one of my sisters till she was adjudged of ripe age, maybe fourteen, maybe as old as sixteen, but as of today she was legally the young Earl of Surrey's wife. Mother, were she living, would not have approved, just as she had not truly approved of my entry into a nunnery at six.

I glanced over at my niece's bridegroom, standing at her side with a rather awkward air. Young, at least. Perhaps nineteen or twenty with a haughty, fine-boned young face and ruffled dark hair that rested upon his jewelled collar. He turned as if sensing my gaze upon him and all of a sudden, a pair of keen, pale-blue, icy eyes met mine…

A strange sensation shot through my body; I clutched my crystal rosary beads till they made marks in my hand. A warm sensation seemed to flood my entire being; I felt giddy and my ears rang. Was I having some sort of religious experience right there in Westminster Abbey, near the bones of Edward the Confessor and generations of my kin?

The unsettling sensation faded as John de Warenne turned his back to me and faced the Bishop who was officiating the marriage. It was replaced by *disappointment*, a knot of despair that knotted my belly, mingled with an unworthy frisson of jealousy toward pallid little Joanna, who would be better playing with dolls than getting married…

The rest of the ceremony passed in a blur. The choir was singing and the fragrance of incense in the censers rushed to my head, giving me a second wave of dizziness. Standing near me, Elizabeth nudged my arm almost imperceptibly. "Are you well, Mary?" she said out of the corner of her mouth.

"Yes…yes, I am. I am weary from travelling, that is all." My voice emerged sharper—and louder—than intended.

A few heads craned around. One of them was John de Warenne's. Again, I beheld those icy eyes, so pale they almost seemed otherworldly, more appropriate to the elves and spirits the common folk believed in than to a human man. Again, my heart beat like the wings of a trammelled bird, and my ears burnt beneath my wimple—thank God in Heaven no one present could see them!

"I think you need to sit," whispered Elizabeth. "Come with me, sister; we have much to catch up on. Can you believe Joan's little Eleanor is the next to wed? Next week!"

"It seems like yesterday she was but a babe," I murmured dazedly, letting Elizabeth guide me between the painted pillars of the Abbey.

As I went out the door into the May sunshine, I halted, half-turning. *He* was there, near my shoulder, circled by his attendants. John, the sunlight shining on the dark waves of his hair, picking out highlights of red and gold. He gave me a tight-lipped little smile; those strange, striking, almost frightening blue eyes were veiled by a haze of black lashes. Then he was gone into the crowds, the bells boomed, shaking the earth like thunder, and my sister was leading me away to a chariot draped with the Royal colours.

I did not see John de Warenne for a few more days. Joanna of Bar was housed with us and that was quite a different matter. Losing the composure she had shown in the Abbey, she could not stop sobbing and refused any consolation. "I don't want to be married!" she wailed.

I felt oddly irritated by her cries and let Elizabeth and Joan do most of the soothing; they, after all, had plenty of experience with unwanted marriages. She would not have to live as John's wife for several years and might change her views completely in that time, as many fickle maidens did. If not, well, she must do her duty, as I had done my duty when I went peaceably to my veiling at St Mary's.

"Mary, you are awfully silent." Joanie approached me, resplendent in her green gown and jewelled cap. I saw myself a ruffled magpie in my black and white, hunched on a stool near her delicate, slippered feet, cawing for the crumbs of an old life long gone. "I have never known you to hold your tongue for so long."

"My head is pounding!" I snapped, and without waiting for either sister to get a word in edge, I rose in a flurry of robes and stalked from the chamber.

The knighting ceremony in Westminster was barred to all females, even royal ones. We heard rumours of the proceedings, though, as the young noblemen poured out of the church after their vigils were over and the dubbing and girding-on of belts of knighthood was complete. The ceremony was supposed to be a mystical affair with the youthful warriors communing with God, but there was much talk on the street of how our brother Edward had crammed a huge party of his compatriots into the nave of the abbey church and irritated the monks with late-night laughter and near-revelry. The holy men could scarce hear their own chanting over the guffaws of their Prince and his friends. Still, that was Edward—joyous and throwing off protocol where he was able. Underneath, he was likely angry too, hence his deliberately inappropriate behaviour—the King had barred

Gaveston from receiving his knighthood at the same time as his son, telling him he would only grant it three days later.

The ladies of the court *were* permitted to attend the grand spectacle of the knighting feast later that evening. I had intended to enter as a Benedictine, in my proper robes and wimple, but seeing my sisters and nieces in gowns as bright as a peacock's plumage, brought a pang to my heart.

As I had done a few times in the past, I drew my rough wool habit over my head and rolled it into a ball, placing it safely in my travelling chest. Then I brought out a deep blue gown, old and not too showy, but wrought of fine eastern silk. I bound it with a silver linked belt Father had given me for Christ's Mass and wound my crystal rosary around the belt-hook. I removed my workaday crucifix of dull brass and replaced it with a finer one on a gold chain—it bore the image of Christ with sapphires for eyes, and the blood-drops on His side inlaid shards of ruby. That was a gift from Mother, long ago, from a Queen to a Princess. And tonight, a princess I would be again. I dared not bare my head, however; I was unmarried on earth and yet wedded to Christ. Also, my hair was shorn—not near to the scalp like some of the other Amesbury nuns, but just above my shoulders—the choice of length had been given to me due to my status so once a year I symbolically cut my hair along with the rest.

The nun's wimple would at least provide some cover, in more ways than one; if word of my attire got back to the Prioress or, worse, dear Cousin Eleanor, the Abbess of Fontevrault, I could argue I had kept some decorum and not forgotten all my vows.

With Joan, her girls, Elizabeth, the drooping Joanna of Bar and Queen Marguerite, we hurried for the banqueting hall. The Queen glanced at me with surprise; she was less used than my sisters to seeing me in clothes other than my religious robes. "Mary, I almost did not recognise you. The deep sapphire of your gown—it brings life to your face. Your skin is smooth as rose petals."

For some reason, her unexpected praise flooded me with warmth. "Thank you for your compliment, Your Grace," I smiled as we walked into the Great Hall to a fanfare of clarions. "It is not often I hear such kind words."

"If I did not know better, I would almost think you had dressed to impress a young man!" laughed the Queen, and I flushed to the roots of my cropped hair. What did Marguerite mean by that? Surely she jested! Whilst it was not unknown for nuns to find sinful pastimes—the first foundation at Amesbury fell into disrepute because the Abbess had three bastard children and her nuns were running riot with local men—no such scandals had happened at the priory in my time, and *I* certainly had never been tempted. *Never...*

Queen Marguerite left our group to ascend the royal dais, and the rest of us took our places at the benches near the high table—standing, rather than sitting since the King had not yet entered the Hall.

A herald blew a trumpet and silence fell as down the central aisle strode Father, his great strides showing all why he was nicknamed Longshanks, the light from a hundred candelabrum turning his long white hair into a cloud of fire. He sat down on the dais beside Marguerite, stern-faced, the warrior king, and beckoned for the banqueters to also be seated, while a crowd of eighty minstrels entertained. They were the best in the land, notably Edward's Welsh musicians Nagary and Amerkyn, William Without Manners, and Pearl In The Eye.

As they played enchanting airs, the newly-made knights filed in, led by my brother Edward, fragrantly scented by the rose- water in which he had ritually bathed the night before and wearing his new golden spurs and sword-belt. With his cheerful, handsome mien and his broad, strong shoulders, he looked every inch a true prince, and the chamber erupted into cheering and horns blared until the windows shuddered in their stone frames. My heart soared with joy for him; pray God, the arguments and tantrums of the past year or so were at an end now that he had assumed a knight's responsibilities.

Once the knights were all seated, the feasting began; the tables groaned beneath trays of scones bursting with whipped jelly, white bread loaves accompanied by pots of salted butter, eels in baked cream, dressed tench and bream, strawberry soup and sugared almonds on silver dishes, capons, pheasants and roasted mallards, a pie shaped like a knight's sword and a peacock complete with its jewelled feathers intact. The food was not the only delight—wine imported from France, Burgundy and Spain flowed freely with cups renewed many times.

Merrily I partook, my dark mood of the previous day lightening, as my head, sore affected by the rich wine, lightened too. I chattered freely to Joanie and Elizabeth, seated on either side, and even warmed to young Joanna of Bar, seeing the vague shadow of Eleanora's face in hers now that I observed her closely.

We talked of old times and how we wished Margaret was here with us, but she seldom travelled abroad anymore and her letters had dwindled in the past year. Her marriage to Jan of Brabant was unhappy—she had told me so herself at Elizabeth's wedding—but the situation had declined further. The Duke had acknowledged his numerous bastards, a pack of boys all called Jan after him, and kept them openly at court, while he carried on with his mistresses in a disrespectful public manner.

So Margaret, having done her marital duty and produced one solitary son, another Jan (although we defiantly called him John), retired to a hunting lodge in the Sonian Forest, which transformed from its humble roots into a mighty stronghold where she might live in peace and quiet.

Our talk of old times and our absent sister faded as a trumpet sounded, followed by yet another, even more strident, and the rhythmic booming of a deep drum. All eyes turned toward the doorways leading into the Hall; the highlight of the evening was about to begin, the grand spectacle our Father had devised in his love of ceremony, of history, of the tales of King Arthur and his Knights.

Two carts draped in silver silks and drawn by teams of brawny squires rolled into the room; atop the carts were golden cages containing full-grown swans with golden chains clasped about their sinuous necks. The great birds flapped their wings and struck at the cage bars with their bills, seeking freedom or at least to smite their gaolers.

The carts ground to a halt before the dais. My Father arose from his throne, like an old King Arthur himself, and he stepped down from the dais, his movements exaggerated, theatrical, knowing all eyes were upon him. Slowly, deliberately, he set his hands upon the bars of the cages; the two birds inside went wild, flailing and fluttering, darting at him with their beaks.

"Today I do swear," cried the King in a thunderous voice that held no trace of wavering, despite his age, "at this gathering of my most noble knights, to bring down the dangerous rebel, the unrightful claimant to Scotland's throne known as Robert the Bruce. When his malice is subdued and he is brought to justice, I will then no more lift my sword in battle, save upon Holy Crusade."

Almost as one, all the new young knights stood up, a shining, noble company. My brother Edward came forth, first amongst them, his visage full of youthful ardour. He faced the swans in their cages and cried out, "I do swear upon this day that Scotland will be brought to heel by the power of my arm and the aid of God Almighty; I will not rest till the deed is done!"

His oath-taking was followed by the rest of the eager knights, all kneeling and swearing before the swans and the King that they would wage war in Scotland and then seek glory upon Crusade in the Holy Land.

At my side, Joanie was almost weeping, carried away by emotion. "Look at our brother, how tall and fine he is. And yet…" She shook her head, staring tearfully toward the flapping swans and the bright company of nobles around them.

"What do you fear, Joan?" I asked, curious.

"Maybe you know little, living away in Amesbury as you do." She turned to me, tears marking her cheeks. "In some ways, our brother is not as other men, and sometimes I fear, I fear what will happen to him!"

"He has become friends with Father once more, Joan. He is full of enthusiasm for feats of arms; maybe he, at last, is growing up as he should."

She shook her head. "Mary, I do not talk of youthful high spirits and wilfulness; we were all prone to such moods at one time, myself included. I speak…of something quite different. Something that could…destroy him."

For all that I was a nun, I was not quite the naïve innocent she clearly thought me. She referred to Gaveston, whom Edward called brother—but whom many believed was far more to him than that. I did not know the truth of the rumours, nor did I wish to; all I knew was that Edward was my brother, and I loved him. "Whatever Edward may be, I am sure he will do his duty. He will be a good King one day."

"Will he?" asked Joanie. Her eyes were bright with tears; she had never before spoken to me so frankly. I felt her hand reach out and clutch mine. "I pray you are right, Mary, for I fear…the day may not be far away." Her voice dropped; what she had done was dangerous, even for a King's daughter. She had come close to predicting our father's death.

I glanced at Father, standing between the caged swans, the knights kneeling before him in a circle. He looked so upright, so full of the flame of life—yet, in the darting light of the flambeaux that had just been lit, there was a new hollowness to his cheeks, his eyes, a slight stoop I had not noticed before, a wasted look to his outstretched hand…

No, *no*, I refused to even think about it—or what Edward's reign might be like after his demise if Joan's fears were correct.

Joanie was drying her eyes on the end of her long veil. She took a deep, shuddering breath. "Tonight, I have spoken foolishly…imprudently. What by Christ was in my head? I…I have not been well, Mary. Pray for me."

I stared at my sister in surprise. Joan appeared the picture of womanly health, her cheeks rosy, her beauty undimmed despite having borne eight children. Yet, like Father, if one observed closely, one could see a pallor to her cheeks—their redness was from cosmetics—and she had grown thinner than she used to be, her collarbones prominent, her waist as tiny as a child's.

"Joan, if you are ill, tell me!"

She shook her head and suddenly smiled, but it was not a smile meant for me. Her husband, Ralph de Monthermer, was walking across the flagstones in our direction. Before the royal dais, the floor was clearing, the knights returning to their benches and the musicians getting into position to play; soon dancing would commence, to last long into the night.

I would get no more out of Joanie. Dark mood descending again, I retired to my bench nursing a goblet of wine. I could not join the dance, being a nun; I was an ungainly dancer who stepped on toes anyway. Watching Joanie and Ralph, and knowing what I knew—or guessed—I felt heartsick. Suddenly I had to leave the smoky hall with its scents of smoke, food, sweat and mingled perfumes.

Escaping into a narrow, poorly-lit corridor, I raced for the freedom and solitude of the herb garden. Taking in gasps of fresh air, I stumbled out amidst the dew-spangled lavender and rosemary bushes. The moon floated above, half-full, a lamp that sent blue-silver light rippling over the spires of Westminster. A breeze, cool, from the north, stroked my face, strangely soothing.

Sitting upon a stone bench, I leant back and closed my eyes. The wine had sorely affected my head; the world was heaving slightly. On the morrow my brow would pound as if a hammer had struck it. Mumbling to myself, I reached up to touched my wimple, which hung slightly askew, a little worse for wear—just like its owner. I wanted it off, to let that silken wind run over my scalp, through my short, blunt-cut hair. No one was around, no one would care; well, maybe God was watching, but He, in his grace, would know I meant no harm…

The wimple came off, fell to the ground. I ran my fingers through my hair, damp with sweat…And gasped, as if I had been caught in a sinful act.

A man was standing in the garden, a black shadow near the door leading into the palace. My heart started to race. What was he doing out here? How dare he spy on me?

A nervous laugh broke from my lips. Probably he was thinking the same about me!

"Whoever you are," I called, "stop your gawping and show yourself."

The figure moved, feet hissing slightly on the dew-drenched grass. A crack of light from the archway behind my seat struck his face—I recognised the man. John de Warenne, who had so recently married my niece Joanna. John with his dark hair and proud mien, with his eyes like chips of ice, so pale they seemed near enough unearthly.

Despite myself, a small gasp tore through parted lips. He was almost the last person I would have expected to encounter here.

"I thought you were a boy," he said. It was certainly not what I expected him to say. "The hair." He gestured to my shorn head.

"What do you expect?" I said tetchily. "I am a nun of the Order of Fontevrault."

"You do not look much like a nun." He grinned, his teeth white diamonds in the gloom.

I snatched up my discarded wimple—but did not attempt to put it back on. "You think I wear this wimple for mere amusement?"

He glanced at the rest of my outfit; the silk dress, the jewelled cross. "I have no idea, my Lady. I did wonder if it was part of a mummer's costume."

"A mummer! I'm the King's daughter! Why do you think I was invited to your wedding to Joanna, my niece? To provide the entertainment?"

He groaned, suddenly pressing his hands to his temples. "My wife, Joanna…no offence, Aunt Mary, but I would rather not speak of my marriage. The union displeases me."

"Why not?" My voice was sharp. "It increases your standing in the world, does it not? Joanna is the granddaughter of a King!"

"She's ten years old!" he said. "And, more than that, she is not to my taste."

I bristled. "You have an offensive tongue, sir!"

"Only if you call honesty offensive." He grinned again, his eyes shining like a wolf's. "Then again, some say I am a brute with no redeeming qualities. A rogue, just like my father William before me. His enemies hated him so much they stabbed him to death after a tournament at Croydon. Your father liked my grandsire, though, and put him in charge in Scotland, telling him, 'He does good business, who rids himself of shite'. The Scottish rebels being the shite, of course."

"My father…you would do well to remember 'my father' is the King of England! And you've insulted his kinswomen more than once tonight."

"You are right—I *am* a beast. Forgive me, if you will." He leaned towards me; I could smell the drink on him. Suddenly he clasped my hand, pressing it to his lips.

It was as if waves of fire burnt me inside out. I gibbered like a loon. "I must go!"

Clutching my crumpled wimple before me like a protective shield, I fled the garden.

"I will see you again, though, won't I?" John de Warenne shouted after me. "The King's extravaganza isn't over yet—isn't there your other niece's marriage to attend? I'm going to have to attend myself, now that I'm part of the family!"

I refused to answer. What an awful, presumptuous young man he was—and yes, *young*; I must have had a good eight years on him.

At my back, the sound of de Warenne's mirth drifted on the wind. Laughing at *me*, at a sad silly nun who had been caught unawares. I did not know whether to feel furious…or disappointed.

Chapter Ten

My niece Eleanor de Clare, age thirteen, was married to Hugh de Spenser the Younger, one of my brother's long-time companions. She was a pretty and biddable girl and one of the King's favourite grandchildren—he supplied her with a handsome dowry of some 2000 pounds. For the wedding, she wore a gown of deep-green silk that had come all the way from Tripoli; it foamed like green waves around her feet, giving the impression that she was rising, like the goddess Venus, from the deep Mediterranean Sea.

As I stood watching the ceremony with Elizabeth and Joanie, I noticed John de Warenne on the other side of the chapel, dutifully hovering alongside the little figure of his new bride, Joanna. He winked at me; I returned what I hoped was an off-putting, black-browed glare. Inside, I was full of tumult; was he mocking me, or was he…*flirtatious*. I knew so little of the ways of men. I had never missed such frivolity, such play between the sexes, and I dared not ask either of my sisters—they would reel in shock that a gentle nun of Amesbury should speak of such earthy things…

A few weeks later, the King decided to move his armies towards Scotland once more. Edward was given command of the royal forces, while Father travelled in a litter with the vanguard. By now, all the family realised that what we feared most was coming. We did not dare guess when but knew it would be soon. It was as if, once the knighting ceremony of the Swans was over and the next generation of warriors chosen, all Father's remaining strength had fled. His hue was yellow; often he clutched his right side in pain. His neck ached as if too weak to hold up his head, and he suffered intermittent flux.

"Ah, Mary…" Queen Marguerite was heartbroken as the last of the marching men vanished into the distance and the banners bearing the Leopards of England were sucked into a dusky gloom. "I fear I shall not see my dearest husband again. I wish he would have stayed at Windsor and let the physicians attend him! But he is stubborn, so stubborn!"

"I know." I wished I could have embraced her to give comfort, but one was not permitted to touch the Queen. "I fear for him, too. Yet, we must think of his own wishes—would he be happy to lie abed with doctors rushing around him while his armies marched to battle? He would see it as dishonourable."

Marguerite bowed her head. "You are right. I speak from my own selfishness. Mary, when your Father is gone, I swear I shall never wed again."

"But you are young! Many will expect you to remarry."

"It matters not what others wish. Edward is all to me. No man can ever match him in my eyes."

I nodded. "Nor mine. I understand."

I remained in London with Marguerite while Joan returned to Clare and Elizabeth travelled up to Lochmaben castle in Scotland, which Father had granted her earlier in the year.

Daily we waited for messages about the King's welfare to come from the north. They arrived in fits and starts and the news was always grave; the progress was slow, the King needed to stop and rest for extended periods along the route. He was having trouble eating and swallowing, and the pains in his legs, neck and belly continued unabated. In a panic, Marguerite sent him casks of pomegranate wine and rose-water shipped from Damascus, along with a stream of doctors armed with possets and potions made of crushed gems, amber, pearls and sea-coral. Nothing helped. Edward I, Hammer of the Scots, was failing.

It seemed Father knew it too. When August arrived, hot and humid, the nights ripped apart by great storms that cleared the air but briefly before the heat built again, he sent a special missive to Marguerite. There were no words of comfort, no niceties, no insistence that he would soon recover. Instead, he consolidated her lands and possessions and set out provisions for her children, including the matter of little Princess Eleanor's dowry.

Seeing this done for the Queen and my baby sister gave me some small comfort. When the worst befell, Marguerite would not suffer financially or lack a place to live.

Despite wishing to stay longer and offer my support, I soon had to leave Marguerite's side; the Prioress Joan had sent a series of increasingly stern letters querying the reasons for my long absence from the convent. An even harsher letter had arrived from Cousin Eleanor at Fontevrault. Some years before, the Prioress of Amesbury had appointed me as a visitatrix, my duties to inspect other nunneries and report back on their strengths and failings. Eleanor threatened to strip away the position—and with it my rights to travel beyond Amesbury—if I did not leave London in short order and go back to the convent.

I had no choice but to depart. Saying my farewells to the Queen, I climbed into a chariot and directed my entourage to head east, not to Amesbury, not quite yet, but to the Shrine of Walsingham and St Edmundsbury. Surely Abbess Eleanor and Prioress Joan could not complain overmuch about that—I was truly going on religious business, to pray for my sire's health and that of sickly little Eleanor.

The abbey church at St Edmundsbury was filled with the scent of incense. Before me stood the shrine of the great martyr, draped in golden cloth and adorned with tributes left by the faithful—gold lozenges, coins, rings, candlesticks, unmounted gemstones…

To my left, on the abbey wall, the candlelight illuminated a huge mural depicting Edmund's martyrdom. Tied to a tree whose roots seemed to dig down to hell and whose boughs scraped at heaven, he writhed in agony as his heathen captors shot him full of sharp-tipped arrows.

He looks like a porcupine, I thought, rather irreligiously, remembering one of the strange spiky beasts once resident at the Woodstock bestiary.

I pushed the sacrilegious image from my head, and prayed harder, especially for my sickly little sister and declining father.

Dear God Almighty, your humble servant Mary, a nun of Fontevrault, thanks you for the safe birth of Princess Eleanor of England...but I ask you, in your Divine majesty and mercy, to gift health on said princess and on Edward King of England, who has served you well and is now afflicted. God...my Father cannot die yet; we need him, England needs him. My brother is truly not yet ready to be King...

Rising from my knees, I began to walk back down the nave of the abbey church, past other pilgrims heading to the shrine. Another wall-painting loomed into view on the other side of the church, under a window filled with incarnadine glass—St Edmund's head, severed after death and guarded by a supernatural wolf. The head had apparently cried '*Here, here, here*!' to those searching for it—and then attached itself back onto Edmund's arrow-riddled body…

In truth, I thought the wolf was more likely about ready to have its supper when the searchers arrived, but that was just another of my unbidden, irreligious thoughts! Nevertheless, the painters had certainly made the guardian wolf ferocious in appearance, with an upstanding ruff of hair, crimson eyes and a slavering mouth filled with daggered teeth…

Hot breath blasted on to my cheek and I jumped in alarm, half expecting a wolf to be running alongside me, giving me a sinister vulpine grin before rending me with its fangs.

But it was no wolf. Nor was it just a silly fancy.

It was a man. A man dressed in a rich dark cloak that swirled around his booted ankles.

A man whose eyes were pale and wolfish, gleaming ice-chip cold between the strands of his wild dark hair.

John de Warenne.

My heart gave a strange, uncomfortable lurch; my ears flamed beneath my wimple. "My lord de Warenne," I said, refusing to meet his probing, mocking gaze. "What a surprise to see you here in St Edmundsbury. What brings you to this holy place?"

"The same as you, my Lady. To pray at Edmund's shrine and ask for his intercession with God."

"Oh? I did not somehow think you were the religious sort, my lord."

"I thought much the same about you, Sister Mary."

Cold anger flooded through me. "I am a nun of Fontevrault, as I told you. How dare you insult my piety?"

"I dare because I'm a rogue, as I told *you*." He stalked around me, circling, his cloak belling, reminding me more than ever of the wolf painted on the wall, but not a holy wolf who helped a decapitated saint find his head, but a predatory one waiting to defile and devour. "Do you know what I prayed for, Lady Mary?"

"I can scarcely imagine." My tone was acidic.

"To be free of my marriage…"

"So…you think you can stand there and insult my niece, Joanna! She has already suffered much in her life, poor child, and I am sure she likes you no better than you like her!"

He shrugged. "I hold no real animosity towards your niece, but I want a wife in the present, not one years from now. In fact, I have one in mind."

"A woman; I should have guessed." I rolled my eyes. "Why did you agree to the marriage then?"

"It was my grandfather's dying wish that I marry into royalty," he grinned. "I agreed at the time. It seemed a good plan at the time. I had not met my sweet Maude then."

"I do not understand why you plague me with your immoralities. I do not wish to know. I am not ignorant, although I am veiled; you can surely keep your harlot as well as my poor niece. That's how many men behave."

"But Maude doesn't want to be a harlot." John flung his head back and laughed.

"Again, no concern of mine." I pushed past him, hurrying toward the door of the abbey church, trying to make eye contact with the monks scurrying past in case I should have to scream for help.

John was behind me, a dark shadow, the snarer, as sinister and beautiful as Satan himself. "I fear I have done you wrong. I did not mean to upset you. I like you, Lady Mary."

"Truly? You have a strange way of showing it, sir. Insulting me, insulting my family…"

"Ah, life should not always be so serious. I did not think you were that serious, Mary. One reason I felt *drawn* to you."

I sputtered. "I think you have imbibed too much wine, my lord. You insult me again!"

"A *serious* nun would not come to court, nor ride with a retinue. A serious nun would not wear a princess' gowns and jewels, or gamble a fortune away…" He halted in his tracks, hands on hips, Lucifer the Lightbearer arisen, the afternoon sun picking red strands from his dark curls and making those strange, too-pale eyes shine like lamps. Sunlight trickled down the sharp straight nose, the carved cheekbones. "Mary, Mary, I am not your enemy. If we never meet again—well, will you play a game of at dice with me? I enjoy a gamble, even as you do. I have heard you are good at dicing."

"I am good," I spat. "I have played since childhood."

"Interesting things they teach princesses! I never knew. Then you will play against me?"

"What is the prize?" I could scarcely believe the words falling from my lips.

He touched the pouch at his belt. "Forty pounds. I am sure you could use it with your Father being away."

Another insult; I reddened, knowing how far in debt I always was. I had no idea my failings had reached so many ears, but then John was 'family' now. He must have heard a great deal of unflattering gossip during the knighting ceremonies in London.

"And what would a nun possess to give you in return?" I regretted those words even as they fell imprudently from my lips, but to my surprise, John's face bore no meaningful leer, no suggestiveness. He merely shrugged.

I reached to my belt, where my crystal rosary was wound about the humble twine belt girding my middle. It was a fine enough piece, but Elizabeth had given me an even finer one at our meeting at Westminster, with red coral against the Evil Eye, and a sprinkling of carnelians, rubies, enamelled gold, and silk tassels.

He saw where my hand rested and nodded. "A fair deal. You will play?"

"Where? I will not make myself look disreputable."

"You stay where, my Lady?"

"The Abbey guest-house, of course. No, you can't go there."

"Whyever not? I am your loving kinsman now, as all the good brothers surely know. It is certainly a more appropriate meeting place than, say, my lodgings at The Cock Inn."

I grimaced. "The Cock Inn. I dare say you are right. I will inform Abbot Thomas that the Earl of Surrey, my dear kinsman, wishes to confer with me in the matter of my niece, the Lady Joanna. All will be out in the open then…save the gambling, of course."

"Of course. I look forward to playing against you, Sister Mary," he said, his lip curling with his usual insolence. Then, with a curt, impolite little bow, John was gone, leaving me in the porch of the abbey church, with the gargoyles on the roofline glaring down and the sky beyond growing thunderous, as if God frowned in anger at his frivolous daughter.

The Abbot was not best pleased by my announcement of the Earl's 'visit' but there was not much he could say; de Warenne and I were indeed kin by marriage, as he well knew. Clearly, he had heard of John's reputation of roguishness before now and was fearful of something scandalous taking place under his roof..

I sat in my guest-house chamber, paintings of the Holy Mother gazing down from the walls with sad eyes, and waited. Would John turn up? As light slipped from the sky outside and the room darkened, I began to think he had cried off. Or was lying drunk in his lodging. Or was rolling around with some whore…

Why did *that* thought bother me so much? That was the kind of man de Warenne was. A rogue, by his own admission.

A feeble knock sounded on the oak door. "Enter," I said, as imperious as any Queen.

A monk with a long, wan face poked his head around the edge of the door. "Uh…um…" he stammered. "Sister Mary, the Earl of Surrey has arrived and requests to speak to you."

"Send him in." I tried to keep my voice steady.

The monk vanished and moments later, John threw open the door and marched in, bold as brass. He smelt of horses and rain; outside the daylight had completely faded and the clouds had opened, disgorging their watery contents over St Edmundsbury. His hair was shiny, wet and curling. I swallowed deeply.

"Greetings, cousin," I said, using familial address, although he was most definitely no cousin of mine. "Come, sit."

I had arranged a table where we might dice. Candles stood all around it in branching candelabrum.

"I have brought my own dice."

I held out my hand, palm up. "I want to see them."

His dark brows shot up into the curled fringe. "You think I would cheat you?"

I shrugged. "If you want to play, you'll do as I ask."

Lips drawn in a tight smile, he reached to his belt-purse and drew out some dice, dropping them one by one into my hand. Carefully I examined them—old, yellowed, wrought from bone.

"Do they pass muster, my Lady?" he queried, voice full of insolence.

"They do," I returned, "but still I would prefer we use mine." I reached to the table and collected up my own set of dice. Mine were made of polished jet from Whitby, black as sin.

"As you wish," said John. "I would not have you believe me a cheat and end up being paraded around the market square with my dice dangling from my neck like some common fairground swindler."

"Wine before we begin?" I inquired, all politeness.

"I would never say no to wine."

I reached for a nearby goblet, rim glittering with gemstones. Filled it, handed it to the Earl. I poured myself a glass too; I felt I would need it. Then I sat down, the gleaming black dice lying before me on the table. "Let us begin. Best of, oh…shall we say a dozen games plus one, Lord John? The one who wins the most times takes all."

"Thirteen, it is. An auspicious number."

"And I…" I smiled, "shall be the Caster in the game."

We played, stopping in between each game to sip our wine, jibing at each other in a way that seemed strangely exhilarating.

"Are you going to keep doing pilgrimages wherever I go?" I drawled.

"Quite possibly…I trust you don't object?"

"I *do* object. I have strong doubts you would be going to these shrines to pray. You're pursuing me for some reason. No, I can't help you get out of your marriage to my niece Joanna."

"You wound me, Lady. As if I would do such a thing." He pressed a hand to his heart as if stabbed. I was quite minded to see if there was a sharp implement around and stab him indeed—not lethally, but somewhere that hurt. Fortunately for John, no such item was at hand.

We continued to play, concentrating as hard as we could, willing the die to fall as we wished. It seemed we were evenly matched, neither one luckier than the other. He would win, then I would, then back again.

"It is strange for me to look across the table at a nun," said John.

"It's strange for me to look across the table at a man!" I laughed.

"I liked you without the wimple. Back in London."

"You said I looked like a boy. Do you prefer boys?" The wine was in my belly now, burning, loosening my tongue—making me stupid.

Anger suddenly blazed in Jon's strange, pale eyes; I'd mortally offended his male pride with my rude, ridiculous comment. "No. As best I know, there is only one man of high rank in this country who prefers the favours of a catamite!"

I understood to whom he referred and was shocked—and then furious. "You could find yourself headless for such talk!"

"Do you threaten me, little nun?" He leaned over, his wine-fumed breath hot in my face, his own visage no longer pleasant but suffused, angry.

"I do not. I just warn you."

His arm swept out in a flash, knocking the dice and their horn container to the tiles. "Enough of this! I am finished with these…these games."

"I win, then!" I cried triumphantly. "You have chosen to surrender the game."

"No, I have not. And I *always* win. Always!"

He was at my side, too fast, too quick, his movement serpent-swift and unexpected. He grasped my wrists, yanking me towards him. His pallid eyes were intense, burning into mine. "You are no true nun, Mary! You are not made for such austerity. You could be free of it, you know…say you were forced to take vows as a child…"

"You've gone mad!" I struggled against him; anger blended with fear. "Let me go."

"I admired you from the moment I first set eyes upon you. You deserve more than to languish in a house of dried-up virgins."

"What would be better? Sinning with the likes of you? When you are married to my…" I found my tongue, and it was sharp. Suddenly I gasped and my eyes widened. A horrible truth struck me. "I know what you are about now! You hope to seduce me so that you can have your marriage to Joanna annulled! You would tell an ecclesiastical court that you had bedded her aunt, thus making your union with her incestuous. You…you BASTARD!"

My hand came up, struck him a glancing blow to the cheek. He staggered back, then reddened, his teeth gritted. His hand reached to his side, fingers clenched—luckily, he had been told to leave weapons outside the abbey precinct.

I drew myself to my full height, which was not much, I had not the long legs of my sire, but the Plantagenet temper was burning in me, making me an enraged giant. "Go!" I ordered. "Leave this place at once. I will decide whether or not to inform my Father the King of your base actions."

"I do not care if you do! I will deny everything! All men know you are a nun of poor habits! Christ's teeth, you are probably not even a virgin, you've likely tupped every monk and passing priest at Amesbury."

"Get out, John," I repeated with firmness. "Get out, you stupid, violent, foul-mouthed little boy."

He grunted like a beast, making my guts curdle. How could I have ever seen anything attractive in him, even for a moment? What a fool I'd been and it had nearly cost me dearly. Very dearly.

Angrily de Warenne stalked to the door, flung it open with a crash. A monk was hovering in the hallway outside; John elbowed him roughly aside as he strode for the exit.

The monk leaned in the doorway, rubbing his sore belly where John's elbow had jabbed.

"You are well, Sister? I take it the Earl lost the game!"

Chapter Eleven

Father was at Lanercost Priory in Cumbria, ailing and unable to make the final push across the border with his army. His physicians, still desperately administering cordials and potions, said he would not be able to travel till spring—if then. News arrived of dissension in the ranks—Humphrey de Bohun, my own sister Elizabeth's husband, left Scotland without the King's permission, accompanied by none other than that infamous popinjay, Piers Gaveston, among others. The reason?—they wanted to join in a tourney.

Father had forbidden tourneys while England was at war.

Needless to say, the King was both incredulous and enraged; he stripped Humphrey and the other deserters of their estates and called for their arrest. Poor Elizabeth, away at her castle of Lochmaben; the property was now held by the crown and her husband under lock and key.

Fortunately, Marguerite, playing the Queen's role of intercessor with both grace and determination, managed to soothe Father's rage in a series of pleading letters. Humphrey and the other foolish knights were soon released from various dungeons and their lands restored.

Leaving Amesbury, I travelled to London in order to visit the Queen and keep apprised of what was happening in the north. Marguerite was desperate to see me; in private, she fretted over Father's failing health and the weakness of little Princess Eleanor, who was so small for her age she looked like a tiny doll.

"You must take her to Amesbury soon, as we agreed," Marguerite said, as we toured the nursery. Eleanor was in the arms of a great buxom nurse but she would not take the breast and was fitful and crying, drawing her legs up beneath her. "She is no stronger. I fear the heat and stink here do her no good. The peace and quiet of the convent will help, I am certain. She is nearly of weaning age…not that she takes much sustenance, poor little soul."

"It will be done soon, then," I reassured Marguerite. "We will do what we can at Amesbury. Sister Infirmarer is highly skilled with mixing tinctures and potions to aid health."

Departing the nursery, the Queen and I headed to the solar. Once inside, Marguerite banished her ladies-in-waiting and the gaggle of musicians playing on lutes and harps for their entertainment. She began to pace the tiles, wringing her hands in distress.

Something was sorely amiss. My heart began to thud against my ribcage. "Your Grace—Marguerite—whatever is wrong?"

"I cannot keep silent any longer," she said, voice shaking. "I have had more news from Lanercost Priory. Your Father and Edward have had a terrible fight. The worst they have ever had."

"Tell me," I breathed, heart sinking.

"It is Gaveston again, Gaveston who caused this grief." Marguerite's eyes glittered with tears. "To think I once interceded for him, on Edward's behalf. I am told Edward walked up to your Father, strutting like a peacock, and told him that he wished to grant the County of Ponthieu, which he received on the death of your sweet, virtuous mother, to his 'dear brother Piers.' Cornwall, too. Cornwall, which has always been held by the royal family!"

Audibly I groaned. Had my brother lost his senses? Important counties were not handed out to friends, no matter how beloved!

"My husband went mad…" Marguerite struggled to contain her emotions; her hands clenched into fists at her sides. "Although weakened by his illness, he sprang from his seat and grasped hold of your brother, tearing the hair from his head in his rage."

I gasped. Many harsh words had been spoken by my Father and many times his Plantagenet temper resulted in broken doors, furniture and even coronets…but he had never physically attacked any of his family in rage before.

Marguerite sat down on a window-seat amid the plump silk-lined cushions and put her head in her hands. "He shook the prince as a terrier shakes a rat, and shouted into his face, 'You baseborn whoreson, you want to give away lands now, you who never gained any!' He then threatened young Edward's inheritance and had him chased from the room into the night…"

"The King will calm down." I knelt by Marguerite's knees on one of the rich rugs—left over from my mother's tenure—that were thrown across the floors in the Queen's Apartments. "He always does. You know that, your Grace."

She glanced up. "Gaveston has been banished to Gascony. Who knows how Prince Edward will behave without his *companion*. What if he resorts to treachery against his father? His sire who is so frail and ill!"

"My brother is foolish but not a simpleton." I tried to reassure the Queen. "He would never go as far as to rise in open rebellion."

But as the shadows of twilight fell outside and the chamber grew dim, I felt my confidence waning along with the light. Edward had shown himself as headstrong and rash, increasingly so—only God knew what he might do next.

After a few weeks, I returned to the convent, taking with me my half-sister Eleanor, even though she was still young enough to have a wetnurse, which was not in our initial agreement. Never mind, what was one more mouth? She soon settled in the priory, and I actually enjoyed mothering the tiny girl, something that had never before come naturally to me. Joanie's daughter, Joanna de Monthermer was completing her novitiate at Amesbury and she, too, was enamoured of her little half-blood aunt, so tiny and frail. We would take her in a basket lined with fleeces down to the strange old warm pool just out of sight of the cloisters and bathe her feet in the waters and show her the odd purple-hued stones that lay in the shallows like jewels waiting to be plucked out for a princess's trousseau.

The peace did not last long, however. One morn, not long after Prime, a rider came to the priory gates, seeking admission. Once Prioress Joan had spoken with him, I was summoned to her offices along with my niece Joanna. As we walked together down the cloister, I squeezed Joanna's hand in mine—I knew this would not be good news. My guess was that the King had expired, age, sickness and frustration over his son and the troublesome Scots taking the ultimate toll.

In the Prioress's office, the messenger stood near the hearth, still cloaked, a tall man with a drooping moustache and slumped shoulders. The Prioress rose as Joanna and I entered the room, her visage sombre and serious. "Sister Mary, Sister Joanna, this courier bears news from Clare in Suffolk."

From Joanie, my sister? Joanna and I gave each other puzzled looks. I had no idea why a message should come from Joan—unless she had decided to remove Joanna from the nunnery before she had taken her final vows. That must be it—she had decided instead on a marriage that would prove more profitable to the Monthermer family. Anger lanced through me; she should have made such a decision long ago, not now, when Joanna was near enough a fully-professed nun, and a good nun I thought she would make.

"Oh, what does Joan bother us with?" I said testily and moved toward the lanky form of the messenger. "Where is the letter from my sister?"

The man's face assumed a pained expression; his mouth worked. Was he simple…or ill? "My…my Lady, there is no letter."

"No letter?" My brow wrinkled, perplexed. "I do not understand…"

"Sister Mary…" Prioress Joan shuffled forward and tugged at my sleeve. "Let the man speak. It is important…"

At my side, Joanna made a frightened noise. "It is one of my sisters or brothers, isn't it? Or my father! He's away fighting the Scots."

"My Lady Joanna." The messenger licked his dry lips. "The message was sent by his Grace Prince Edward!"

"Edward!" I cried. "Now I am more confused than ever."

The man drew back his cloak, showing me that he indeed wore my brother's household badge, a Golden Tower. "His

Grace the Prince has been at Clare; he was in southern England seeing my lord Gaveston away into exile…" He hesitated. "He made a detour to the east when he heard grave tidings…the Lady Joan de Monthermer died suddenly two weeks past."

Beside me, Joanna gave a cry and staggered backwards; I thought she might crumple to the floor. The Prioress caught her, gently lowered her to the flagstones. "Do not weep, child. Although this is a terrible shock, it is as God wills—he has a greater purpose for your mother. We will say prayers for her soul here at Amesbury until eternity."

I stumbled towards the messenger. "I beg you tell me what happened. Last I heard from Joan she was well…" My voice trailed off as I remembered how vague and strange Joan had been when we met at court. As if she knew or suspected something she dared not tell.

"I am told her Ladyship had grown thin and frail, Sister Mary," said the man, "but she laughed it off, said it was only because she was busy. Then suddenly, she was in great pain from within, and although the doctors were summoned immediately, within a few days she was dead."

Joanna made a hiccoughing sob on the floor.

I crossed myself. "Jesu have mercy on my sister, Joan de Monthermer. God assoil her." My mind flew back to our childhood days—when we fought like cat and dog over dolls, dresses, anything at all and nothing. I had thought her a little snob, brought up separately in Ponthieu; she had seen me as a frumpy brat who behaved more like a hoyden than a princess. Then, as adulthood progressed, our rivalries slowly waned and we saw each other as different people—as sisters, not rivals.

Unchecked, tears ran down my cheeks. Christ knows, I would miss Joan. And Father…how would Father, sick and ill, filled with rage and grief over Edward's behaviour, take the news of his daughter's unexpected death?

The Queen called for me to attend her in Northampton. Marguerite was also grief-stricken at learning of Joanie's death. Kissing little Eleanor farewell—she peered up from her oakwood cradle and smiled a weak, gummy smile—I set out toward the Midlands with a retinue of twenty-four stout men who protected me and kept my baggage carts rolling over the uneven roads.

The weather was atrocious, mirroring my unhappy mood, and I was glad when the walls of Northampton appeared through the rainy murk on the horizon. The town was one of strategic importance and the site of many past parliaments; as I drew closer, I could see the Royal Standard and Marguerite's own banner flying over the top of the four-square castle keep.

Riding down from the Market Square, past St Peter's church, which was used by the castle garrison, a few curious onlookers emerged from timber-framed buildings to gaze at the small nun passing by with the large entourage. Not many, though; the rain was still driving down, running through the clogged gutters, washing away butchers' offal and animal dung. The whole town smelt, in turns, wet and rank.

Ahead of me loomed the castle gatehouse—a welcoming sight, the metal-studded gates open, ready for my entrance. Raindrops slapping my exposed face and making me spit water like a gargoyle perched on a church roofline, I pushed my sodden mare forward over the bridge and clattered into the bailey.

The steward led me to a chamber in the Queen's apartments where, to my delight, a bath scented with exotic oils was waiting. Marguerite was always a thoughtful hostess. Stripping off my damp and now rather smelly woollen robes, I sank into the steaming water, gasping for a moment as the warmth hit my clawed, frozen fingers and toes, making them give a throb of pain.

When I was done, I slipped into a long, dark robe from one of my chests. Not nun's garb, but sombre enough to draw little attention. Not that anyone, other than Marguerite's damosels, would see me and most knew me and my ways anyway.

The Queen was waiting in her warm, homely bedchamber. The scent of spiced wine floated on the air. The furnishings were lavish, parts of the stonework here quite new; Grandmama Eleanor and King Henry had gutted the old apartments and rebuilt them, adding upper chambers and a small chapel. There was a royal nursery too for my little half-brothers Edmund and Thomas, now six and seven years old.

Marguerite looked even more careworn and tense that when I had seen her last. Dismissing her ladies, she beckoned me to her side and gestured to the full goblets on the side table and the sweetmeats next to them on a silvered tray. "Thank you for coming, Mary. Perhaps together we can find strength. Poor Joan; I cannot believe she is gone. She always defied your father, but he loved her the more for it, secretly. She reminded him…of himself."

Tears misted my eyes. "What will happen now, I wonder? Her son Gilbert is in his minority still."

She nodded and then reached out a hand to clasp mine. "I have heard from your sire, praise be to God. He wants you to have two manors to hold in trust for the boy. You will profit by this, naturally. Ralph de Monthermer shall look after the rest; he will need the money as his earldom has now passed to Gilbert."

"Father is very kind," I said, "and he remembers that I am always short of money." My tone was full of shame; I seldom thought of my debts, other than when I asked for help paying them, but today, in the wake of Joan's demise, it was fitting I indulge in rare contemplation

"Prince Edward is on his way to Northampton," said Marguerite. "I believe he wants to grieve with his dear sister whom he sees so little. He is also likely afraid to go north after his terrible fight with his father—although it is his duty to go."

"He is making the situation worse!" I cried, suddenly angry at Edward. I banged down my goblet, slopping wine. "It seems every move he makes is wrong…"

"I know," said Marguerite, and her expression was bleak, "but we must work with him, Mary. For I fear soon he will be King."

Edward arrived with little pomp and ceremony, which pleased me, for I do not think I could have borne it had he come to town amidst a festive atmosphere. Silently he slipped into Northampton Castle and asked for me to attend him in his quarters.

As I entered his private chamber, I thought how he looked the worse for wear; he still wore his mud-speckled garments from the road and his long golden hair was matted from the wind. Bags hung under his eyes, ageing him, robbing him of some of his handsomeness.

"Mary…" He gathered me in an unexpected embrace.

Despite myself, I began to weep on his muscular shoulder. "Why? Why was I not informed of Joanie's death sooner? I could have been at her burial, said my farewells at the graveside…I am always left out!"

He shook his head. "Mary, even I was informed late. With Ralph de Monthermer far away, it seems Joanie's whole household was frozen with grief and did not act as they should have. Do not blame them, though—they loved her well and were deeply grieved."

"Tell me of her burial, Edward." I wiped away my tears with a sleeve. "You were there—tell me. I pray it was worthy of a woman of her rank."

"It was, fear not. First, she was laid in state within the castle chapel. She looked so fair, Mary—as if she just slept. Her hair was brushed out in a cloud around her, like the locks of a princess in an old tale. Candles burnt around her bier and her women wept and wailed as if the world was at an end…Several of her children were beside her, praying for her immortal soul; they bore her death as bravely as they might."

"Poor Joanna, her daughter and my companion at Amesbury—she sorrowed greatly since she was not able to attend the funeral with her siblings." I thought of my niece slumped to the floor in St Mary's, Prioress Joan de Gene kneeling beside her limp form, trying vainly to give comfort. She had lain sick from grief for days after, barely able to rise from her pallet.

Edward bowed his leonine head. "After my arrival, Joan's body was borne from the castle to Clare Priory on a great funeral hearse. Once inside the Priory, the hearse was carried into the Chapel of St Vincent where a Requiem Mass took place. And so our sister was laid to rest. God rest her sweet but proud soul."

I thought of Joanie there, lying amidst the incense smoke, spirit flying up with the angels to God's Throne. Knowing my sister, she would likely argue with those angels for precedence on the way up and make sure she had the greatest fanfare of any soul ascending to heaven that day…

The thought brought a sad little smile to my lips, but Edward spoilt the moment by turning to me with a pained expression and saying, "Such a difficult time for all of us, Mary. Joan gone…and I have suffered doubly, with my dear brother Piers cruelly sent across the sea to exile. Father is so unreasonable. I had only wanted to fit him out as a lord of his stature deserves."

Anger bubbled within me. "*Cornwall*, Edward. You wanted to give him Cornwall. That was Uncle Edmund's earldom. It is meant for the King's family. Father no doubt wishes it for Thomas—your half-brother. As for Ponthieu, yes, that is yours by inheritance but it is earmarked to be the dower lands of Isabella of France, your future wife. "

Edward waved his hand in the air as if swatting at a fly; it was as if he had not heard a word I'd spoken. "Maybe I was a…a little over-eager, but my friend is all to me. I pray he will survive alone without my company…"

"I am sure he will be just fine," I said through gritted teeth, uncharitably wishing for a shipwreck or a fall from a horse. Unholy, for a nun, yes—but then Cousin Eleanor had always said I was an unworthy Bride of Christ.

"I have done what I can for him." Edward stalked to the nearby window, staring out at the rain-drenched bailey with a distant, mournful expression. "I've given him two buckram tunics and some tapestries to brighten his new abode and make him think of me each time he gazes on them. I've also sent swans and herons for his table so he will not go without."

"Yes, we cannot have dear Piers starving to death," I said with sarcasm. Edward failed to notice; I swear I saw dampness in his eyes.

"He had so few men with him," he mumbled, filled with misery. "I sent one of my yeomen, John de Baldwyn, on the journey with six grooms; I pray that will be enough to give Piers adequate protection against rogues and brigands. I'll need to get some horses to my Perrot as well; he will need them for tournaments."

"Tournaments!" I blurted. "You know how Father feels about tournaments. Edward, this is unworthy…"

He was not listening; his thoughts were elsewhere—with Piers Gaveston. Distant Piers who was probably even now enjoying himself somewhere in France on my brother's largesse.

I brooded, upset and angered. Joan was dead, Father likely dying…and Edward was worried about his 'brother's' ability to show off in a tournament. "When are you returning to Scotland to assist the King?" I asked coldly.

The naming of 'Scotland' seemed to bring Edward back to reality. Taking a deep breath, he glanced guiltily in my direction. "Oh…oh soon, very soon. I cannot escape it." He frowned as I continued to glare in silence. "Do not worry, sister, I know my duty."

"I pray you do, Edward," I said quietly. "I will go to the chapel now and pray that God guides you in the right direction."

Turning on my heel, I left my brother standing in the window embrasure, a tall figure ringed in faded gold by the faint sunlight spiking through stormy clouds in the sky beyond.

Edward left Northampton, his aspect sullen and gloomy. I was glad to see him head north at last. Marguerite and I turned our attention to the children, Thomas and Edmund. Thomas had just had his seventh birthday and was clattering about the keep with a new wooden sword. Edmund was just happy to trundle along in his boisterous brother's shadow and eat 'Gingembras' shaped like little men with rough dough heads and stubby arms and legs. Father used to send Mama Gingembras when he was away; it not only tasted delightful but was medicinal, easing a queasy stomach.

I was tempted to ask my smallest brother if he might share his sweetbread for my belly was tied in a sick knot, for all that I tried to go about my daily routine. I sensed that something was about to happen and that we stood on the edge of great change, maybe even ruin. I prayed more diligently than I had ever done before that Father's strength would return. But there was no denying the truth: he was an old man whose life had revolved around battle and hardships. His time was nearly done.

On the 1st of July, the air was hot, humid, almost unbreathable. At night a massive thunderstorm broke over Northampton. Sheets of lightning turned the sky as bright as day and rain lashed down in torrents. Winds howled with demonic fury, and in the nursery my little brothers, imaginations fired by the storm, wailed and wept in fright.

Unable to sleep, I stood in my chamber away from the shuttered window, where the lurid storm-light crept through the cracks. The booms and blasts were as loud as siege engines assailing a fortress; it was as if the heavens had opened to attack us.

An irrational fear filled me and I flung myself on my *prie-dieu,* clutching my rosary beads until my knuckles turned white—and I heard, above the roars of angry heaven, the sound of the great wheels that drew up and released the drawbridge squealing as they ground into motion.

Plucking up my courage, I stumbled to the window and unfastened the shutter. The wind nearly snatched the wooden frame from my hand; rain blasted into my face. Lightning speared the bruised clouds boiling over the castle's ramparts. Squinting against the blast of the gale, I gazed down into the inner bailey. Messengers on horseback, being greeted by men bearing torches that wavered and dipped as the storm snatched at the flames.

I retreated inside my room, slamming the shutter again and putting my back against it. Was this the moment I had dreaded for so long? Was my Father dead, finally fallen to the ravages of age and care?

A brisk knock sounded on my chamber door. Yes…yes, it had to be. Hurling on a robe, I shot the bolt back and opened the door a crack. One of Marguerite's ladies stood outside, trembling in her shift. "My Lady Mary? You are to come at once, Sister. The Queen is requesting your presence."

"I will come immediately," I mumbled, mouth acid. I dragged on my imported silk slippers—a gift from Father last Christ's Mass—and hurried out into the corridor after the woman.

I found the Queen's apartments in turmoil; servants were packing her gowns and other possessions in travelling chests while she overlooked the removal of her goods. When she saw me, she grasped my sleeve and dragged me behind a painted screen. "Is he…is he?" I stammered.

"No," she said, "Edward lives yet, but his physicians say the situation is grave."

A reprieve then, even if only a brief one. I closed my eyes. "You are going north then, your Grace?"

She shook her head, her face pinched with pain and regret. "Too far, too dangerous—and maybe no time. I thought, perhaps, to pray for God's intercession at St Thomas' Shrine in Canterbury and St Thomas Hale's Shrine at Dover Priory. I am taking the boys, Mary; will you accompany me?"

"I will," I said. "Father is old but his will is iron. If God decides to help, perhaps he may yet be saved."

Our chariot flew down into the south of England, bumping and crashing over ruts and hollows in the road. Inside, the little Princes, sickened by the rolling motion of the carriage, cried as they heaved into bowls held up to their faces by their nurses. I gripped the edge of the window, watching grimly as villages and towns flew past, a blur of church spires, bridges and shocked faces.

At last, beyond all hope, the massive spires of Canterbury cathedral appeared, glimmering in the gloom of early twilight. As our retinue filed into the cathedral close, monks, priests and prelates poured out to greet the royal party.

The Prior, Henry de Eastry, stood on the steps leading to the Cathedral door, mouth opening to begin what he intended to be a speech of welcome. It should have been the Archbishop, Robert Winchelsea rather than de Eastry—but Robert had quarrelled bitterly with Father and was currently in exile in Bordeaux.

The Queen, climbing from the chariot, waved a hand at him in an unusually imperious gesture. Her worn face showed her strain. "No time, de Eastry! I must go to the Shrine of St Thomas at once!"

Henry de Eastry reddened but wisely did not question; the grave news of Father's worsening illness had already reached Canterbury. "Come with me, your Grace," he said, extending a white-clad arm in our direction.

Marguerite and I rushed into the dark nave of the cathedral, the nurses dragging the young princes behind us. Our feet clattering on the tiles, we followed the Prior into Trinity Chapel, under the ornate dome of the Corona, named for the shard of skull sheared off the vengeful swords by St Thomas's murderers.

Before our faces rose the Saint's Shrine, his sacred bloody tunic lying over it, the offerings of Kings and nobles glimmering in the gloom on the surface and around the polished marble pillars that supported it. A reliquary casket stood as the centrepiece, holding the sanctified bones; it was wrought of gilt copper and enamelled in blue; on the sides, engravings showed the tragic scene of St Thomas' martyrdom. The knights pressed forward, blades ready; God's hand stretched down from the firmament to whisk the saint straight to Heaven.

Marguerite fell to her knees, pressing her face against the base of the shrine and pressing her lips reverently to the chill stone. I could hear her praying, the words coming in rushed, gasping breaths.

I sank down beside her, doing likewise, trying to envision the blessed Saint as he sat near to God's Throne, and asking for his intercession. *I beg you, St Thomas. Father is old but England needs him still. Grant him strength, grant him freedom from affliction and death for but a little longer...*

Marguerite pulled back; her headdress was askew, her long golden-brown curls hanging, tears shining on her cheeks. "Madam..." Prior de Eastry went to assist her but again she waved him away.

"I need no help, Prior. I know what I must do. Thomas, Edmund, you must now come forth and kiss the good St Thomas's tomb while you pray for the health of your father."

I moved aside and the nurses pushed the boys forward. Both looked terrified, particularly the younger. Although this was a holy place, I understood how it might seem intimidating, with cowled monks and priests sweeping round, their mother in a frenzy of fear, and the fluttering candles creating vast, sinister shadows that leapt and swayed as if concealing devils who would sweep them to hell if they acted improperly in God's House.

"Do not be afraid, children." I attempted to give them some comfort. "The only presence here is that of God and the most blessed of Saints. You will come to no harm, I promise."

Hastily the boys knelt on the foot of the shrine, kissing the stone underneath and trying not to dishonour themselves by grimacing. Out of the corner of my eye, I noticed Edmund wipe his mouth afterwards then, realising I was watching, look terrified as if he expected I might point at him and shout '*Blasphemer!*'" Instead, I gave him a reassuring little smile and mouthed, "All is well."

Henry de Eastry approached Marguerite. "I worry for you, your Grace. I beg you retire to the comforts of the Bishop's Palace, where I may counsel you and hopefully bring you some spiritual peace before the next step of your journey."

The Queen shook her head. "My thanks, but I cannot halt. We must press on to Dover Priory as planned."

The Prior wrung his hands together in concern. "Your Grace, the hour is late. You have children to think of, the noble princes…" He gestured toward my half-brothers, who stood hand-in-hand, fairly leaning on each other with exhaustion.

"I have my husband the King to think of," said Marguerite coolly, "and the future of England."

De Eastry looked thoughtful but still worried. "I do understand the urgency, your Grace, and yet…"

"I may be but a woman but I am tougher than I appear, I assure you," retorted Marguerite, "and my boys—they are the sons of a King—the greatest of Kings. What kind of sons would they be if they lay abed, sucking on sweetmeats, while their father was in peril?"

The Prior knew he had lost; there was nothing more he could say to dissuade the determined Queen from the final leg of her pilgrimage. "As you wish, your Grace," he murmured in a low voice and stood aside.

"Lady Mary, are you ready to journey on?" Marguerite gazed at me as if afraid I might side with de Eastry and beg her to stay the night in Canterbury.

She need not have feared. My desire was nigh as great as hers. "I am ready," I replied, taking a deep breath.

Darkness still lay over the land when we reached Dover, although the rim of the eastern sky was growing red. The Priory of St Mary and St Martin of the New Work stood in the heart of town, with the sea a flat stretch of shadow beyond, its centre lit by the faint chip of a westering moon. On the cliff above the town, the huge bastion of the castle thrust into the shadows like a clenched fist, proclaiming its might; it was the very gateway to England and had never fallen to invaders. Before its feet, the white cliffs that formed the country's seaward façade gleamed a pale white-blue; several flocks of seabirds, waking with the first trace of dawn, screeched and flapped along the cliff-face, their wings shining with an eerie glamour as if they were those of ascendant angels…

The monks were anticipating the arrival of the Queen and her children. The pointed arches of the monastery were golden with the light of many tall torches burning on poles. The light fell on the grand carvings decorating the building's western exterior—the Blessed Virgin with outstretched arms, the warrior Saint Martin seated upon a horse and dividing his mantle with a sword. A beggar in rags crouched near the hooves of Martin's steed, arms uplifted to receive the gift of the divided cloak.

The Prior, Robert de Whittaker, a youngish man with a drawn, austere face emerged to greet the party; quickly, he ushered the Queen, the boys and me into the Priory compound, while his servants dealt with the horses and our attendants.

"I have received advance news of your urgent need, your Grace," he said to the Queen as we dashed down the night-bound cloisters lit only by the hazy glow of cresset lamps nestled in the corners. "All is ready at the shrine, as you would wish."

He guided us into the Priory church, where a nimbus-wreathed image of Christ resting on a woolly cloud gazed benevolently down from the chancel arch. Up near the high altar, a multitude of candelabrum stood in a ring, arms branching out like the limbs of so many trees, hot pools of wax gathering in cups beneath them.

Here was the shrine of St Thomas de Hale…Well, the Pope had not yet beatified him, so he was not truly a saint yet, but many folk called him so already, for miracles had taken place at his tomb. As saints went, he was unusual in that he had lived not so long ago; his martyrdom had taken place but twelve years prior, when a French raiding party had attacked Dover and broken into the Priory seeking plunder. While all the other monks fled, Thomas, who was old and infirm, remained in his dormitory. Finding him, the brigands took hold of the old man and tortured him to get him to reveal the Priory's wealth; despite his agony, he refused, and so they impaled him on their swords. Miracles at his gravesite began shortly thereafter.

The Queen entered the ring of light from the candelabrum; the little princes and I followed. St Thomas's tomb was a low altar tomb graved with a rough effigy; coins and other offerings lay atop it, glinting in the candlelight. Marguerite went down on her knees and I knelt beside her, my small half-brothers near me. Poor mites, they looked near enough to falling over with exhaustion, but they were aware of how much this meant to their mother, and they behaved as young princes should.

I cast up my eyes towards Heaven, invoking the old man who had been put to death so cruelly within his own church. *I pray you hear me, holy St Thomas; I am your sister Mary, a fellow Benedictine. Evil men smote you down when you were old and frail; I pray you lend strength to another man of august age who we need to lead us against our enemies...*

When we had finished, all energy seemed to leave Marguerite. Ashen-cheeked, she slumped against a wall. Young Edmund began to whimper.

I took control. We had done what we could; we had prayed to two saints and asked for their intercession with God. It was time to rest, even if only for a short while.

"Prior Robert, I trust accommodation is ready for the Queen and her sons?" I asked, quite sternly.

De Whittaker nodded. "Yes, the Brothers will show you..."

Marguerite still looked faint and dizzy; her steps were feeble, tottering. Striding from the church, I called to the ladies-in-waiting and nursemaids who had accompanied us on our journey. "Here, come at once. Attend to the Queen! She needs assistance. You nurses, come as well. The Princes are long past their bedtime."

The monks' countenances showed traces of horror as three non-royal, non-veiled women in linen servant's caps rushed into their church, followed by two others in flowing gowns but they held their peace. The ladies-in-waiting saw to Marguerite, fanning her grey face and escorting her out of the church, while the nurses laid hold of their small charges and departed for the comfort of the guest house.

Weary to the bone, I followed after, my feet dragging on the scrubbed-clean tiles. Heraldic badges flashed underfoot in a blur; my eyes were so bleary from exhaustion, I could scarcely make the images out. A sick headache gripped my temples. We had done what we set off to do…but would it be enough?

As it turned out, the answer was no. The very next day, only a few miles out upon the long ride home, our company was met by armoured men in royal livery, their faces grim and stony beneath their helmets. A herald rode amongst them, wearing mourning colours, his head bare of any helm.

"Oh, no…" Marguerite breathed beside me in our chariot. It was inappropriate but in the dark between our cushions, I gave her hand a sympathetic squeeze.

We both knew what was coming.

Marguerite called for a halt and she alighted from the chariot, slow as an old woman, looking as if she might snap and break. The herald, his hair tousled by the wind and his face gaunt with strain, sank down on one knee.

"Your Grace, I bring ill news from the North. His Grace, King Edward, is dead. Long live King Edward, Second of that name. Long live the King."

"I thank you for bearing this news to me so swiftly, although it is grievous news indeed," said Marguerite courteously. "You shall be rewarded for your troubles. But first, tell me what you can of my dearest lord's last hours."

The herald took a deep breath. "He died as a great warrior—the greatest. For days before his demise, rumours had spread abroad amongst the Scots that he was already dead. This filled him with endless rage…"

"I can imagine!" said the Queen, laughing through threatened tears.

"He insisted on faring north, not in a litter but mounted on his warhorse. However, by the time the army reached Burgh-on-Sands, he was gravely ill and could go no further. He was carried to a bed where he called for a priest, knowing that the end was nigh. At the same time, he cried out that his son must carry on the Scottish wars, bearing his bones before his horse on a pall as a warning to the enemy. Even as he declined further, he would not rest despite the advice of the doctors. Calling for his armour, he struggled to rise and ready himself for battle. His squires ran to assist him—and he fell back dead in their arms."

Marguerite bit her lip, trying to contain her grief. "Carry his bones into battle? How pagan that sounds. Jesu, did anyone dare heed that last request? His bones, naked of flesh; no proper burial? I cannot bear the thought…"

The herald shook his head. "Fear not, Madam. His Grace the new King took charge at once. He said his Grace was to be embalmed, chested and sent south for burial with his forebears."

Marguerite flinched to hear the herald talk of Father being prepared for the grave, but I could tell she was also much relieved that his last furious cry about soldiers bearing his bones to war had gone unheeded. In the past, men who died abroad were sometimes boiled in great vats until the flesh fell away and then had their bones shipped home in a box, but Edward was a great King and it seemed only right that he should enter Heaven whole.

The Queen turned in my direction. "He shall be buried in Westminster near your mother, Queen Eleanor, and your grandfather King Henry. I will wait for him to return to me, on his final journey."

"Where will you go while you wait?"

"Back to Northampton, behind the stout walls of the castle. I will feel safe in such a stronghold. Once men find out that the King is dead, unrest might spread throughout the land; such is the way of things. I must protect my children. Will you come with me, Mary?"

Weary and heartsick, I passed a hand across my eyes, every muscle in my body aching. "No, Marguerite, I must return to Amesbury to rest awhile—to pray for my Father's soul and to grieve as a daughter should. I will attend the burial, however, when all is arranged at Westminster."

Nothing would prevent me from saying my last farewell.

In August, the funeral hearse bearing my Father's body reached Waltham Abbey, where he lay in state for several days before the high altar, surrounded by pots of burning incense and tall tallow candles. Not far away stood one of the twelve beautiful crosses he had designed in Mama's memory; her image, crowned and robed, gazed out of austere stone, smiling gently. I prayed, somewhere, they were together. My Father, I will not lie, could be a hard man, a violent man given to fits of temper—but he had loved Mother dearly, and Marguerite after her, and all his children, even though we often frustrated him to fury. He even loved my brother Edward, who thought Father despised him; I swear his hostility was only from vexation, and the knowledge of the burdens Edward would one day bear as King.

After Waltham, his body was borne on to its final resting place in Westminster where alongside Queen Marguerite, Elizabeth and I watched our Father, the King of England, laid to rest in a severe stone tomb that bore no effigy at the King's own request. A stern tomb for a strong lord who was the Hammer of the Scots. Elizabeth wept openly; as the youngest daughter, Father had doted on her most and there was a special closeness between them. Margaret, far overseas, had not come—and Edward, my brother, England's new King, was still in Scotland.

Elizabeth turned to me, tears shining on her cheeks. "What shall become of us?" she said tremulously. "He was our protector, our guardian; sometimes he seemed invincible."

I tried to put a brave face on it. "Life will never be as before, yet still the sun will rise and set and the flowers bloom in Spring. We have a new young King on the throne—our brother, who loves us."

Elizabeth stared down at the intricate Cosmati tiles beneath her shoes. "Does he anymore, Mary? Or is his love all for Gaveston now?"

"Hush, it is not a fitting thing to speak about in this holy place," I chided—but in truth, the same troubled thoughts had passed through my mind many a time.

Change was coming, and I sensed it was unlikely to favour the remaining daughters of a dead monarch.

Chapter Twelve

February of 1308 was cold but the skies were clear and sunny. "It's a good omen, surely," murmured Elizabeth as we stood beneath a spangled canopy fringed with pearls raised upon the bustling docks at Dover. Out in the distance, the sun shone on wave-caps in the Channel, emblazoning them with gold; the seabirds were crying and wheeling as they dived through the riggings of ships in the harbour.

"We can but hope—and put our trust in the Lord," I said.

I felt distinctly uneasy. Edward was returning to England after marrying twelve-year-old Isabella of France in Boulogne-sur-Mer—and while he was away, he had made Piers Gaveston Regent of England. Regent! Our Father was no doubt spinning in that sombre grey tomb in Westminster. Mutterings of shock and anger had sounded amongst the barons; all the nobles were dismayed by such an unorthodox turn of events. Edward remained oblivious to their concerns, or just did not care—he had given Cornwall to Piers, just as he had always wanted, evoking the strongest response from Father, and he had even gone as far as to marry his friend to Joanie's daughter, Meg de Clare. Gaveston was now wed into our family; we were stuck with him for good or ill, and his children, should he have any, would be of the blood royal.

Gaveston was here at Dover with our party, his handsome dark face keen as he watched the royal ships dock and the gangplank lower from the first, the one which bore the King. Piers was dressed in a fabulous peacock-hued cloak and wore a circlet studied with rubies that spelt out his name—as if any of us could forget it.

On the ship's deck, I spied Edward's leonine golden head, a riot of long curls. He ascended the gangplank with great speed, hurrying toward Pier Gaveston without a glance towards any others, while all the assembled courtiers, guards, bishops and barons gaped in utter astonishment.

I frowned and so did Elizabeth. Where was his little bride Isabella? She should have been at her husband's side—Edward should have presented the new Queen of England to her people.

"What has happened to our new Queen?" Elizabeth murmured, drawing closer to me. "This is most peculiar! Unless..." She grimaced, remembering events from a distant past. "Unless she was as stubborn as I was in my youth and refused to accompany her husband!"

"I pray Isabella is well," I said, my unease growing. "Remember the fate of the little Maid of Norway, who was once set to marry our brother?"

But I did not truly think the new little Queen was ill...or worse...or even just a demanding chit like my sister, choosing her own time of departure for married life. There was no sign of sobriety in my brother. Edward seemed happy; he was smiling as he strode across the docks, his face bright as the sun hanging overhead in the sky. But then his attention seemed focused on one only...

"Piers!" he cried, and he flung his arms about his friend and embraced him as if they had spent years apart, kissing his cheek with a fervour that made many avert their eyes or whisper behind their hands.

Face reddening, I cringed. How did Edward not realise that people would be scandalised? No one, save his confessor, would much care, in all honesty, what went on within his royal bedchamber—but to show such public affection! It could, and would, cause a scandal.

"Piers," Edward continued, holding the Gascon at arm's length, "My dearest Brother! I have missed you so. Your good service to me while I was away shall not be forgotten."

Forgotten? Edward had clearly forgotten *something*—his new wife.

The little Queen-to-be, Isabella, was coming up behind him on the harbourside, having arrived separately in her own ship, *The Margaret of Westminster*. Uncertain and shy, her cheeks glowed bright pink with embarrassment in the wan February sunlight. Her French attendants thronged behind her, their faces pinched with outrage at the perceived slight on their mistress.

Isabella was beautiful. Her father was known as 'The Fair' and he had clearly passed his handsome appearance to his daughter. Tall for her age, her hair fell in golden waves to her hips, while her face was a perfect oval with wide, deep eyes and a small pert chin. She bore a slight resemblance to my sister Joanie, which made me feel a little sad.

Gracefully, Isabella walked along the quay, her dress of blue and gold, the colours of France, floating around her ankles, her cloak of red velvet lined with yellow sindon belling in the stiff breeze off the water. Despite her youth and the unorthodox way in which she ended up presenting herself to her people, she bore herself with great courage and fortitude, acting as if nothing untoward had happened.

Edward finally appeared to have remembered he had a wife and watched her graceful procession with pride for a moment or two. That gave me a jolt of hope—maybe when Isabella had gained womanlier attributes in a year or two, he would become more enamoured of her. Whatever his relationship with Piers Gaveston, I knew there were women in his life too. Maybe Isabella could use feminine wiles to overtake the Gascon in his affections.

But then Edward appeared to grow bored. Piers was leaning on his arm, whispering in his ear. The young King laughed at whatever witticism his favourite had pronounced and waved dismissively in Isabella's direction. His new wife was hurried away to a waiting chariot, which swiftly set out upon the road. Edward then climbed upon his own mount and Gaveston swung up onto the saddle of his own steed, and together they rode off deep in conversation, as if there were no others in all the world.

Elizabeth and I were left with the other ladies of the court and our guards and personal attendants. We had no time to think further on our brother's actions because suddenly we heard a voice calling us. Through the crowd pushed a familiar figure, one we had not seen for years. It was our sister Margaret, dear Megot, home from Brabant for Edward's Coronation.

Embracing joyously, we laughed and wept there on the docks of Dover while activity swirled around us; other great ladies being loaded into carriages, chests full of clothing and jewels for Isabella and her companions being stacked high on wains.

Margaret suddenly looked startled, glancing around through the chaos on all sides. "Sisters! At this rate, we shall be left here alone on the harbourside, prey for pirates and lustful French sailors! We must go with the others. Shall we all ride in my chariot, as if we were still children at Langley?"

"Of course!" said Elizabeth. "We have so much to talk about—much more exciting things than when we were girls."

"No fighting over toys or sweetmeats then?"

My sisters laughed and I laughed too, but it was clear to me our positions in life had changed with Father's demise. At one time, we would have taken precedence, as the King's daughters; we would have left the quay before any of the other nobles were permitted to move. Now, we were just the children of a dead monarch, still important ladies, the new King's sisters, but our place in future events was now limited. Once we bathed in the light of our parents' glory; now we had stepped aside into the shade.

Edward and Isabella's Coronation took place several weeks later when February was almost done. Originally scheduled for earlier in the month, it had to be postponed for there was still much upheaval over Piers, and the Archbishop of Canterbury was not only still in exile but also gravely ill. As it turned out, the Bishop of Winchester would have to stand in for the occasion.

In many men's eyes, it was not the best start to Edward's reign. Along with Elizabeth and Margaret, I took my place in Westminster Abbey on a tiered platform erected in the crossing of the nave, which was reserved for royalty and great magnates and their wives. Highborn ladies thronged at our backs, resplendent in their best gowns and headdresses. The Dowager

Queen Marguerite had a special seat of prominence, along with little Edmund and Thomas—the very least Edward could grant them, since he had stolen Thomas' expected birthright, the Duchy of Cornwall, to bestow on Piers. Other guests in our high wooden stand included royals from the French court, Isabella's Uncle Louis, and her brother, Charles. Margaret's straying husband Jan of Brabant was also there, eyeing the fairest women with ill-disguised lechery, while around him gathered numerous other dukes and counts of high renown, a riot of rich colours, silks, velvets and glimmering gemstones.

At the far end of Westminster Abbey, a door banged open with unexpected suddenness, allowing extra torchlight to flood into the dim building, momentarily blinding the assembly. As the organ began to thunder, its great vibrations making the floor quake, the Coronation procession began, stately and glorious, although it came from the back of the church rather than through the expected western doors. I guessed there was such a crush of onlookers in the square outside that the procession had slipped in through a secret way in order to protect the King and his little Queen from harm.

First strode the imposing figure of Humphrey de Bohun, Elizabeth's husband, clad in traditional cloth of gold with the royal sceptre held firmly before him. At his heels walked Thomas, Earl of Lancaster, bearing Curtana, Sword of Mercy, and the Earls of Warwick and Lincoln holding the other Swords of State. Several paces behind, another group of lords bore the royal vestments on a board draped in checked cloth: deep, unsmiling Hugh de Spenser, Thom de Vere, son of the earl of Oxford, Edmund Fitzalan, the Earl of Arundel, and darkly handsome Roger Mortimer of Wigmore, of whom I knew but little save that he was high in Edward's esteem. Then came the Treasurer and the Chancellor, carrying the paten of St Edward the Confessor's Chalice and the holy Chalice itself, and William Marshall who had been appointed to bear the Spurs.

After these worthies had passed towards the high altar, there was a little gap in the procession. Heads craned around—soon the King and Queen must arrive. Suddenly a gasp went through the assembled nobles standing nearest the postern door and I strained my eyes through the flare of a thousand torches. A figure *was* approaching, but it was not the King.

It was Piers Gaveston holding the royal crown on a tasselled cushion, dressed as if this was *his* Coronation and not my brother's. Great lords on this day were permitted to wear cloth-of-gold but Gaveston had outdone them all and pushed the boundaries once more—he wore a long robe of finest silk dyed royal purple, the hue permitted only to kings, which was dotted all over by hundreds upon hundreds of pearls glowing like tiny moons in the warm vibrancy of the torches and candles.

The communal gasp of surprise was followed by angry, shocked whispers that echoed through the Abbey; to my ears, it sounded as if a hundred snakes hissed in fury. Gaveston in royal purple, like a King…Gaveston who was not of high nobility, who was not even English-born, bearing the symbol of monarchy in his unworthy, bejewelled hands!

Piers paused, hesitating—or was he truly like a peacock displaying his finery, taunting the great lords who despised him? An impish smile curved his sensuous mouth before he moved on, a haze of vivid purple and gold.

Edward and Isabella finally appeared. My brother wore a leaf-green robe and black hose; he was barefoot as he crossed the Abbey floor. He was certainly less eye-catching than Gaveston and even the Queen in her vivid red-and-yellow cloak.

The ceremony began. I was so unnerved by Piers' behaviour and extravagant garments that I was fitful and restive; my head began to pound as a great headache tormented me. The organ was still booming out, the sound crashing in upon my temples; I began to sweat furiously beneath my habit.

However, all went as it should until it came time for Edward to have his gilt spurs affixed to his heels. Isabella's uncle Charles, a Prince of France, knelt reverently to perform this solemn, ceremonial duty. Almost immediately up strode Piers, who fell to his knees with a flourish before my brother and fastened on the right spur. Again, hissing and muttering ran through the congregation. Piers Gaveston now dared to put himself on the level of a prince…

Edward seemed unaffected, or unaware, that the crowd inside the Abbey was shocked and scandalised. He proceeded, calm and unflushed, to take his Coronation Oath and be anointed with the Holy Chrism that he would have to wear in his hair for the next week.

As he was guided to the throne and sat upon it, robed in majesty, sceptre in hand and crown gleaming on his brow, the *Ta Deums* rang out and Piers made to lead the procession out of the church—but not before, whether by chance or design, he wrested the sword Curtana from Thomas of Lancaster and strode toward the west door with it. The mutters of anger in the onlookers began to turn to shouts of utter rage. He had gone too far. One baron raced forward, cursing him and uttering threats; the man was swordless, luckily for Piers, and was dragged back into the throng by his fellows who held him firm.

The Abbey was now in disarray. Edward was still receiving homage from the last of the nobles and had not seen the hostile reaction to his friend.

Suddenly from near the high altar, there was a terrific crash that made the ladies scream in fright and men shout out in alarm. One huge panel of the hastily built stand had come adrift and crashed down—a few moments later, I saw monks scurrying and men running, dragging a limp, bloodied figure between them.

"Oh no…" Elizabeth pressed her hand to her mouth in abject horror. "Look, Mary, some poor soul is sore hurt, maybe even dead. This…this is not how Edward's Coronation should have been!"

She was right. Our brother deserved to experience the decorum and nobility of his ancestors, not this…*circus*. Still, the ceremony was complete; Edward was anointed and crowned. He was beyond a doubt King of England and beautiful little Isabella, dignified and regal as she was fair, was Queen. Hopefully, the upcoming Coronation banquet would make up for the irregularities in the Coronation itself.

It could not be any worse, I told myself, as I exited Westminster Abbey with Megot and Elizabeth and walked, escorted by attendants, across the square with its ornate central fountain gushing rich wine for the celebration.

How I was wrong.

The banqueting hall was full of starving and disgruntled lords and ladies of the court. We could all smell food cooking from the temporary kitchens set up in the lee of the Palace walls, but nothing had arrived on our trenchers…and it had been hours since we had left the Abbey. The delay gave men time to get thoroughly drunk and to comment, with imprudent loudness, on the new tapestries that decorated the hall by Edward's order. Most of them bore the Leopards of England as one might expect—but the rest? They were the Arms of Piers Gaveston, six eaglets, open-beaked, looking as thirsty for attention as their Gascon owner. As if that was not bad enough, there was not one tapestry that bore the Arms of the new Queen Isabella. It was a horrible slight, and the faces of the French nobility were thunderous.

At last, to everyone's relief, a horn was blown and an announcement bellowed by a herald. The King and Queen were coming—and that meant the food was almost certainly ready for serving.

Edward sat down under his canopy of estate, golden and magnificent, and for a moment my heart lifted. For all his faults, he was my brother and I loved him dearly. Isabella was guided to a seat beside him and wine poured for both, and as they drank together, I felt another glimmer of hope…but then, as a shadow crosses the sun, into the chamber sidled Gaveston, still wearing his purple and pearls.

Edward's face lit up at the sight of his companion and he gestured him over to his throne, where a bench was drawn up for Piers alone. A wine goblet found its way into Piers' hand and the two men began to talk animatedly—and intimately—together. Isabella was, again, forgotten—and worse, Edward's broad back was turned toward her. I knew my brother; this was his usual thoughtlessness, not a deliberate snub, but it was dreadfully damaging and set the gossips whispering. The French nobles looked even more outraged; Isabella's uncles rose from their benches once and moved briskly towards the doors, but then appeared to think better of the action and returned, glowering, to their seats.

The food was coming, after all, and I doubted a single person in the chamber was not famished by now.

Finally, the servers arrived, bearing the first course on great gilt platters. The first sign I had that anything was wrong came from their faces; they were either white as chalk or flushed with embarrassment. With almost indecent haste, they unloaded their burdens onto the bleached linen tablecloths.

The feasters stared for a moment, then poked at the fare with their knives in dismay.

Seated near me while her husband Humphrey attended the King, Elizabeth gave a startled exclamation. "Mary, this must be a jest! Surely, it is. Look, just look…and smell…" She made a gagging noise and pressed a kerchief to her lips in distress.

The food was awful. The pastries were cold, half-baked, oozing rancid cod livers. The gravy on the baked eels was over-spiced, making them nigh inedible. The green sauce bathing the loach was the hue of poison and smelt like venom too.

The hall descended into silence. Some folk picked at the platters; most just drank more wine. Edward appeared not to notice, nor did Gaveston, who had badgered Edward into letting him oversee the preparations for the feast.

The next course was brought out; gazes turned hopefully to the new array of delicacies. The dishes were, alas, no better than the first. The meat tiles looked as if some fat cook had accidentally sat upon them while the blancmange was deflated and unappetising. The broth had been over-boiled until only gluey dark froth clung to the sides of the serving bowl.

Now the dark mutterings I had heard in the Abbey began to waft throughout the hall. Several barons looked fairly murderous.

"I cannot believe this is happening!" I murmured, clutching my eating-knife in my fist. I shot Piers Gaveston a daggered gaze and half-wondered if I should prove myself my father's daughter and stab the miscreant. No one would suspect a Benedictine nun capable of such an act. But I could not hurt Edward—and had no wish to spend the rest of my days locked up in the Tower.

"There is still one more course to come," muttered Elizabeth, an air of desperation in her voice. "Surely *that* one cannot fail as the others have!"

The final course of the banquet finally arrived. Frumenty like pus in a rancorous wound, venison tough as an old man's worn boots, and a raft of coloured jellies fashioned into castles and lions, which slumped into piles of wobbling ruin even as the servers set them upon the trestle tables.

"This is outrageous!" Red-faced from imbibing too much wine, Henry de Lacey, the Earl of Lincoln, smashed his goblet down in the midst of one of the collapsed jellies, sending dollops of green and red slush flying over the feasters. The ladies screeched and dabbed angrily at their stained gowns.

On the dais, the King and Gaveston ceased their conversation and turned sharply to face the angry Earl.

Piers let his keen, heavy-lidded gaze travel up and down de Lacey, a broad, hefty man whose golden belt rested on a protrusive stomach that strained against his samite tunic. "Is there aught amiss?" he asked in a lazy, vaguely mocking voice.

"You know what it is!" De Lacey thundered, waving his jelly-smeared fist. "You were supposed to oversee the banquet, but it is clear to all men that you spent most of the time preening in a mirror instead, admiring your pretty face and your inappropriate purple robes. In your incompetence, you've allowed them to feed us pigs' swill!"

Gaveston smirked, his gaze fastening on the Earl's stomach, which roiled about under his garments like one of the unfortunate jellies while he raged. "I do not think the lack of sustenance will do you much harm for one night *Burst Belly*."

A hush fell over the feasters. Somewhere a plate clattered onto the rush-strewn floor. De Lacey's mouth worked; I thought he might froth in the manner of a mad dog. "You insolent bastard!" he roared when he found his tongue. "I demand satisfaction for that insult!"

Behind the Earl, a little titter of laughter came from the benches. Mirth was inappropriate but none could deny that Earl was, well...*rotund.*

Edward faced de Lacey, mouth pursed in annoyance. "Come now, Henry, calm yourself. Perrot made just a jest, didn't you?"

Piers smirked. "Of *course* it was but a jest. I had no idea the Earl of Lincoln lacked a sense of humour."

"See, Henry?" The King smiled down at the crimson-hued Burst Belly—I mean, Henry De Lacey. "No evil was meant. I think you should apologise to Piers."

"Apologise to that cur? Never!" I thought de Lacey might have an apoplectic fit on the spot and fall foaming in the rushes.

The Earl of Warwick, Guy de Beauchamp, rose from his seat and hastened to Henry de Lacey's side. A formidable warrior who my father had held in high esteem, he turned to the King with grave, frowning countenance. "Your Grace, I must agree with Earl de Lacey. The jest was uncalled for and has ruined the dignity of this occasion."

Pier Gaveston snorted in derision. "Dignity! What would you know of that—you, the Black Dog of Arden, who walks around like a monstrous shadow, snarling at all he meets."

Guy of Warwick's eyes ignited and his hand went to his belt, although he wore no sword, this being a time of supposed peace and unity. "Mock all you like, jackanapes, but one day you may learn that this 'Black Dog' has teeth that can bite."

The King began to look displeased. The rest of the hall was in an uproar. Someone, in drunken pique, flung a pie. It squelched into the benches assembled for the French dignitaries. Angry cries arose and men leapt to their feet, stances pugnacious.

Seeing the tempers in the chamber about to ignite, Edward acted, his own displeasure apparent on his features. "Enough! The banquet is over. I shall depart with my Queen and my dearest brother, Piers. I bid you all do the same."

He gathered up his rich robes with an angry motion and stalked from the chamber, Piers and a few other sycophants trailing at his heels. Queen Isabella was left alone for an instant, expression full of startlement, then she too rose, beckoning for her scandalised French ladies, and followed her husband from the hall.

The Coronation feast was truly over, the lords of England angry, the French insulted, the food close to inedible. A most unhappy start indeed to my brother's reign.

Margaret was returning to Brabant with her husband, Duke Jan. She said her farewells to me and Elizabeth as we gathered together in Westminster courtyard. She appeared very solemn, and the unforgiving sunlight picked out lines on her face I had not noticed by torchlight. Mad merry Megot was gone forever.

"I think..." she began and her voice was tremulous, "that I shall not ever stand upon England's shores again."

"Do not say that, Megot!" cried Elizabeth.

Margaret clasped her hand warmly. "Time passes and all things change, Elizabeth. Father, Mother, both are gone. It is not the same."

"But our brother Edward is King. He still cares for us; you know he does."

"He does...but he is not a young boy anymore, the young boy who played with a camel and begged Joan to send her best greyhound to father puppies on his favourite bitch, the boy who loved watching mummer's troupes and would have leapt on stage with them had he been allowed, the boy who enjoyed cutting wood alongside peasants and partaking in other sports below his station. He is the King now, and what may have seemed endearing in his youth is perhaps not so wonderful now. I am fearful for him, sister, and for England. What I have seen these past few days worries me, and I would rather dwell far away in the tower I have built, with its lakes and walks, away from any unrest."

Elizabeth looked crestfallen. "You have a brave husband who cares for you and fair-faced children," said Margaret gently. "Be content with that, and remember me in your prayers."

Finally, Megot turned to me. "Mary, will you not wish me well?"

"I will always do so, through thick and thin." I embraced her in a quick hug.

Her eyes darkened as a cloud scudded over the sun shining over London. "If I give you one word of advice, Mary—I would stay far from court if I were you. I know it is your wish to travel but here…I see a nest of vipers breeding, and I would not see you impaled upon their fangs. There are those who would drag our family down to ignominy to further themselves, of this I am certain."

I thought of John de Warenne and how he had attempted to seduce me at St Edmundsbury. I had noticed him strutting about at the Coronation Feast, my poor niece Joan a cowed, unhappy figure at his side; he had cast me a piercing look that savoured of malice. Yes, the vipers *were* breeding, and even good men turning to treachery when faced with the arrogance and pridefulness of Piers Gaveston—and my brother's lack of discretion in his dealings with his favourite.

"I will take your words into account, Megot," I said a small voice.

My fingers took hers in a final farewell squeeze, and then she took her leave. Her back was straight, her shoulders squared, her veil a cloud about her slender frame. She did not glance back.

With my entourage around me for protection, I rode in my chariot towards Amesbury, mulling in my mind all that had befallen at Edward's Coronation. As we passed through a dense beech-wood near Clarendon Palace, we suddenly found ourselves surrounded by a group of five rag-clad rogues bearing drawn longbows.

I had a few brawny lads serving as guards and was sure they could take these miscreants down but I would rather handle the matter peaceably, if possible, and avert any bloodshed on either side. Sternly, I ordered my men to keep their weapons sheathed.

The outlaws, or rather hapless vagrants pretending to be such, circled my company like a pack of hungry wolves.

"Who's in that fancy carriage?" leered a great fat oaf with missing front teeth and hair resembling an orange bird's nest.

Hidden behind the curtain in the chariot window, my inclination was to shout, "I am Mary of Woodstock, daughter of Edward, King of England!' and so I would have done many years before.

But now all had changed; Father was not alive to protect me just by the power of his name. Carefully, I twitched the velvet curtain aside and leaned out of the window, revealing my rather rumpled nun's wimple. "It is no one of note. Only a humble nun from the Priory of St Mary in Amesbury."

The rogues looked crestfallen when they saw me. "Ah, how can it be just a nun, riding in that fancy chariot?" moaned the fat one to a scrawny companion. "D'you think she has chalices and plate tucked away in there?"

"I have only the clothes upon my back, it's all I own," I lied, grateful that the wains bearing my clothing chests and other goods were still waiting to depart London. I had wanted to return to Amesbury without delay so had left the carters to deal with the return of my items.

"What about gold crosses or rosaries?" another thug said, trying to affect a menacing air—difficult, since he was wearing a most silly battered pink cap that looked like a wart on his head. "Hand 'em over, sister."

The scrawny man nudged the last speaker in the ribs. "You can't rob a bloody nun, Wat! You'll burn in hell."

Master Wart-Cap glowered at his friend. "What you on about, Jem…"

"Thou shalt not steal," I intoned in a dry voice. "One of God's Commandments. But if you rip my paltry rosary beads from me, fear not—I shall still pray for your soul when it descends into the lake of burning fire. When the devils ram their hot pitchforks into your…"

"Enough!" Wart-Cap seemed to think about my words, lowering his bow and scratching furiously at the scurfy pate beneath his headgear as if trying to activate his dull wits. His skin-and-bones companion, jigging nervously from foot to foot, elbowed him again. "Told you…you can't rob a nun! Let's go! Nothing worth a scrap over here."

Scowling, Wart-Cap backed away from my carriage. "Sorry, then, Sister," he muttered, and he tipped his battered cap as if he hadn't just contemplated robbing me, but was only wishing me a good day. "Our bleedin' luck that the only person to come along this way is a goddamned penniless nun!"

With that, the inept little band of thieves melted back into the trees with not a single blow struck on either side.

I stared at the leaves fluttering in the wake of the ruffians and breathed deeply in relief. Sometimes it was not so bad to wear the veil, even if it had not been my choice to do so. Indeed, suddenly I longed for the peace and quiet of St Mary's, for its white walls set near the flowing Avon where mysterious purple stones glowed like regal jewels and kingfishers and cranes waded through the waters. Where my little half-sister Eleanor waited with her nurses, her smiling round infant face full of delight to see her kinswoman return.

"Ride on to Amesbury!" Leaning further from the chariot window, I called out to my grooms, my guards, my attendants. "Ride on as quick as you might, good fellows—to bed and board, to prayer and solitude—to home!"

Epilogue

LATE 1326

I am waiting, waiting in the nuns' herb garden amidst winter-blighted bushes and empty, fallow beds. A monk is coming hence to meet me—no, I have *not* broken my vows of chastity—the meeting is one of business. The monk is Nicholas Trevet, and his purpose in coming to Amesbury is to show me the book he has written of the history of the Plantagenet family. Composed at my request, it is to pay special attention to all that happened within my father's glorious reign.

I am quite excited yet saddened too, for any mentions of my brother Edward, will not be happy ones, I fear. He is no longer King; his lords rose against him and now he languishes in Berkeley Castle, an unhappy prisoner, his future beneath a dark cloud.

Leaning back on my stone seat, I think of the years since Edward's disastrous Coronation. Ruined food…then a ruined reign. Gaveston had been exiled but like a boil on one's buttock, he returned time and time again, puffed up and causing more grief.

Until he was killed, murdered at last by the bite of one of the men he jeered at, 'Black Dog' Warwick, who had him dragged to Blacklow Hill and hacked to death by two sword-wielding Welshmen. His body lay on the ground unburied for days but eventually found its way to Edward—he interred his friend at Langley in a fine marble tomb. My great niece, Gaveston's small daughter Joan by Meg de Clare, was permanently placed into my care at Amesbury.

I shed no tears for Gaveston, that is for certain, nor even for the devastation my brother must have felt at his loss; I had my own grief to deal with at the time. My little half-sister Eleanor had died a few months before Piers; her health had never improved, even with the ministrations of the nuns and physicians sent by Marguerite. She died age five and was taken, at her mother's request, for burial at Beaulieu Abbey.

Marguerite was gone now too; a winter ague contracted at Marlborough robbed her of life, and clad in a Franciscan habit, she was buried at Christ Church in London, a House of the Greyfriars which she had endowed in her lifetime. And Elizabeth, I must not forget my dear younger sister; she has also gone to Christ's arms. Her last pregnancy killed her; the child, a girl named Isabel, died the same day as her mother. At least she was spared the death of her husband, Humphrey, who was killed in a horrible manner at Boroughbridge, caught up in a rebellion against the King. Reports said a spear thrust from beneath a bridge sliced through his intestines as he led a battle-charge, and his dying screams unnerved his forces so much they panicked and a bloody rout ensued.

As for my own affairs, court life was no longer my joy and had not been for some years. When Edward was newly crowned, I attended court on and off, becoming quite companionable with Queen Isabella, who as I predicted grew into a great beauty that Edward could not resist, despite his infatuation with Piers. She soon fell with child; in total, my brother and his Queen produced four healthy, fair children, with a son, Edward of Windsor, who shows great promise for the future.

But over the years Isabella also grew ruthless, even hard; it might have gone differently for her marriage and for the kingdom once Piers was dead, but rather than coming to rely on his wife, Edward sought solace with another of his favourites—this time, Hugh de Spenser. Hugh, always manipulative, quickly became overbearing and oppressive—far worse than Gaveston in many ways. Once again, England was in turmoil because of Edward's unwise friendships.

This time the Queen rebelled in the strongest way, taking Roger Mortimer of Wigmore as her stalwart supporter against her husband. Mortimer was sent to the Tower for his part in the barons' revolt against de Spenser but he escaped and fled to France, where Isabella joined him in plotting against Edward's rule. Returning with an army, they hunted down my brother who was wandering like a lost soul in Wales, his supporters nigh all gone—and it was from there he was taken to imprisonment in Berkeley Castle.

As for the Queen and Roger Mortimer, men claim he is her lover, and I do not doubt this is so; but whatever Mortimer is to Isabella of France, as it stands now, he is as good as King in the minority of my nephew, Edward.

I want no more of these intrigues—my life as a visitatrix to various nunneries is enough now, that and looking after my young kinswomen, my cousin Isabel of Lancaster, my nieces Joanna and Eleanor, and briefly my unfortunate niece Elizabeth, one of Joan's daughters, who fled to Amesbury, a pregnant widow, seeking help against Edward, who was pressuring her to marry Roger Damary, a man she loathed. Sadly, I could not protect her from my brother's selfish whim; she was delivered of a girl-child, Isabella, here at Amesbury only weeks before Edward forced her into a union with Damary. I took her and Cousin Isabel on pilgrimage to Canterbury to cheer her; we all wept together at Becket's Shrine over my brother's growing cruelty and oppression.

Yet…yet I still loved him, missed the boy who had played with the camel at Langley, who had the common touch; my heart was broken after news of his final fall and imprisonment reached me. It should have been so different…Glory had turn to squalor.

A noise in the corridor made me turn my head; I squinted into the weak wintry sunlight shining through an archway. Was it the monk, Trevet at last? He was late, and the chill of the day made me long for both fire and sustenance.

A shadow fell over the flagstones. Prior Richard Greenborough, a stout man with three massive chins, waddled towards me, accompanied by the elderly Nicholas Trevet, his kindly face smiling within his cowl. I sat up to attention, casting off my sleepy memories.

Prior Greenborough extended a wrinkled hand. "Sister, your expected guest, Brother Nicholas Trevet, has arrived to see you."

I rose; I came to just under Trevet's clean-shaven chin. "I welcome you to Amesbury yet again, Brother Nicholas. Is it done? Is the work I commissioned complete?"

Trevet beamed at me; I noted his hands shook a little as he reached beneath his robe and brought out an unbound manuscript wrapped in a protective covering of soft leather. "Sister Mary, it is done to the best of my humble ability. I thank you for allowing me this opportunity. From my youngest days, I have always wished to write a history, a history of the great Kings of England…"

"Well, my Father was certainly a great King," I said with a hint of pride. "Shall we retire to a suitable place? The Scriptorium? I will have a look at your work and tell you what I think."

The book was a glorious thing.

Annales sex regum Angliae qui a comitibus Andegavensibus originem traxerunt, In it my tales of Father and Mother leapt from the page; descriptions of the King with his fierce, drooping eye and shining aureole of white hair in old age, the fantastical story of how Mama sucked venom from his wound when he was poisoned by a Saracen's scimitar during a Crusade, the terrifying tale of how the pair of them escaped the great fire at Winchester and how my sire fell hundreds of feet when a castle tower cracked open like an over-ripe fruit—and lived when others did not.

However, having wallowed in memories both fair and foul for several hours, I felt quite exhausted by the time I reached the end of the manuscript, and almost *empty* inside. Especially knowing how it had ended for my brother Edward; his ultimate fate still undecided, his rule and his Queen's bed usurped by Roger Mortimer.

Brother Nickolas must have seen the sorrow and exhaustion etched in my face, for he drew closer to me and gave me a smile; it was a nice smile, a gentle smile; in his youth he might have been a handsome man, the son of a Somerset knight before he joined the Dominicans and became a noted scholar.

"Sister. You look as if you have had enough for the day. But before you rest your eyes and mind, there is something you must see!"

He brought out a single manuscript page he had held back from the rest and laid it out before me. I looked and tears came to my eyes, but I hastily wiped them away and began to laugh. He had written me, the least of my father's daughters, into his tome, with a great deal of flattery: *The fourth daughter was Dame Mary, who wedded herself unto the high king in heaven. And in so much as it is truly said of her and notably this worthy text of holy scripture: optimam partem elegit ipsi Maria, que non auferetur ab ea. That is as much to say "As Mary has chosen the best party to her, the which shall not be done away from her."*

"Very bold!" I said. "The Gospel of Luke, where Christ defends the Blessed Virgin to Martha."

A little troubled frown crossed his clear brow. "Are you offended, Sister? Do you think the passage inappropriate? I will change it if you…"

"Do not," I said hastily. "I like it, for all its boldness."

And indeed I did. Appropriate or not, boldness and non-conformity was the hue of my life as both Princess and Nun.

I handed the manuscript back to the pleased-looking Nicholas Trevet. "Shall we go dine?" I said to him. "I have private quarters in the nunnery. I will show you the bed my father gave me long ago—it's a bit shabby now, the hangings rather moth-eaten…"

Trevet's normally calm and beatific face was a picture of horror at my suggestion. He thought I was inviting him in for sinful pleasures!

I began to laugh, giddy with delight at his discomfiture. I was no sinner, but not a good nun. I would never, ever change.

Historical Notes:

Mary is another of the missing 'royal ladies' of Amesbury. Her grave, like those of her grandmother, Eleanor of Provence and distant cousin Eleanor of Brittany, now lies lost somewhere on the site of the destroyed priory, a victim of the Reformation.

I decided to write her story as a happier 'lighter' tale than some of my other novels on medieval women, because in some ways she was quite remarkable. It is absolutely true she behaved as a princess as much as a nun. She went to court, attended her sisters' weddings and her brother's Coronation; she gambled, rode about the countryside with a huge entourage, and there was a question about whether she had an affair with John de Warenne, Earl of Surrey—although the rumour only came out after her death, and was probably invented so that John could get rid of his wife, Mary's niece. But she really had no vocation as a nun, so who knows?

Occasionally, for narrative flow I have moved events a little closer together than they were in reality or juggled them slightly. Mary's encounter with John is invented (although there may have been one!) as is the one with outlaws on the way back to Amesbury. All the other main events including the disastrous Coronation banquet are based on actual events of the period. Nicholas Trevet did indeed write a book containing life events of Edward I, almost certainly dictated to him by Mary, but their meeting most likely took place some years earlier than it does in The Princess Nun.

For more information on Mary and her family, these books were a great help:

Daughters of Chivalry by Kelcey Wilson-Lee
Eleanor of Castile: The Shadow Queen by Sara Cockerill
Edward II: The Unconventional King by Kathryn Warner.

If you've enjoyed this book, please consider purchasing one of my others AND PLEASE LEAVE A REVIEW IF YOU CAN!

MEDIEVAL BABES SERIES:

MY FAIR LADY: ELEANOR OF PROVENCE, HENRY III'S LOST QUEEN

MISTRESS OF THE MAZE: Rosamund Clifford, Mistress of Henry II

THE CAPTIVE PRINCESS: Eleanor of Brittany, sister of the murdered Arthur, a prisoner of King John.

THE WHITE ROSE RENT: The short life of Katherine, illegitimate daughter of Richard III

RICHARD III:

I, RICHARD PLANTAGENET I: TANTE LE DESIREE. Richard in his own first-person perspective, as Duke of Gloucester

I, RICHARD PLANTAGENET II: LOYAULTE ME LIE. Second part of Richard's story, told in 1st person. The mystery of the Princes, the tragedy of Bosworth

A MAN WHO WOULD BE KING. First person account of Henry Stafford, Duke of Buckingham suspect in the murder of the Princes

SACRED KING—Historical fantasy in which Richard III enters a fantastical afterlife and is 'returned to the world' in a Leicester carpark

WHITE ROSES, GOLDEN SUNNES. Collection of short stories about Richard III and his family.

ROBIN HOOD:

THE HOOD GAME: RISE OF THE GREENWOOD KING. Robyn wins the Hood in an ancient midwinter rite and goes to fight the Sheriff and Sir Guy.

THE HOOD GAME; SHADOW OF THE BRAZEN HEAD. The Sheriff hunts Robyn and the outlaws using an animated prophetic brass head. And there's a new girl in the forest…

STONEHENGE:

THE STONEHENGE SAGA. Huge epic of the Bronze Age. Ritual, war, love and death. A prehistoric GAME OF STONES.

OTHER:

MY NAME IS NOT MIDNIGHT. Dystopian fantasy about a young girl in an alternate world Canada striving against the evil Sestren.

A DANCE THROUGH TIME. Time travel romance. Isabella falls through a decayed stage into Victorian times.

THE IRISH IMMIGRANT GIRL. Based on a true story. Young Mary leaves Ireland to seek work…but things don't go as expected.

Made in the USA
Columbia, SC
02 April 2022